# SHAWE RUCKUS

# A Chinese REMEDY

**First published in Great Britain in 2021**
**Copyright © Shawe Ruckus**
The moral right of the author has been asserted.
All rights reserved.

Editing, Design, typesetting and publishing by UK Book Publishing
**www.ukbookpublishing.com**
**ISBN: 978-1-914195-59-4**

# CHAPTER 1

## 2015 April Fool's Day

*W*hen fate runs against your favour, you could choke on your own spit, Joyce Peng thought as she bit down on the eco-straw and slowly drained her yuzu tea.

All was still well when she had left her apartment that morning. The sun dancing high in the sky made her feel that London was the right choice.

How quickly things changed.

She clicked her tongue, picked up her diary, found the current date, and wrote in the left page margin.

*Even the LSE could not escape a manufactured risk.*

A piece of paper fell out of the pages.

She picked it up. It was the ticket to the play she had seen earlier that day – *A View from the Bridge.*

Joyce frowned. She vaguely recalled that something had gone wrong halfway through the play at Wyndham's Theatre. She'd heard an emergency power supply operating, but she was too into the play to pay any attention. It was only on her way home that she noticed that the usually teeming Zara shop was empty. That in itself was puzzling.

*Something's wrong.*

There were no passers-by on the streets, no customers in the shops, and no police roaming around.

She feared the worst and quickly found her way back to the entrance of her apartment. Joyce swiped her key card several times, but, to her consternation, the electric door never responded.

It finally dawned on her that there had been a massive power outage.

She wasn't worried at first. She went to her favourite spot on Bow Street for spaghetti all'astice. The maître d' informed her with regret that the restaurant was temporarily closed because of a fire in Holborn.

She wandered lonely as a child.

By five-thirty p.m., Joyce's stomach was giving her constant trouble. Her medication had left her feeling groggy.

She searched for food, store by store. The fire had even paralysed the cash tills at Pret a Manger, making the simple act of paying for a bottle of water impossible.

The only good news was that the Crown Café on the Strand was still open. It was a family-run Portuguese restaurant that she had frequented during her university years. She helped herself to two portions of coronation chicken sandwich and a jam doughnut.

Once Joyce had settled the bill with the restaurant, she took out her phone. It took her a while to find the contact number of her property manager.

The call connected after some campy music, and she heard a man talking. "Hello, David Carter at NP Properties. How can I help you?"

"Well…" she explained, "I'm a resident of your flat on Kean Street, number five, actually. It seems that the power is out in the building. I can't open the entrance door with my key card, and no one was at the front desk. Do you have any idea what is going on?"

"A moment, please," the man said slowly. "Let me pull up your file."

Another minute of unstimulating music filled her wait.

"Miss…Peng? I thought you were still away. Now that you are back… uhh…let's see. How can I help again?"

Joyce sighed and recounted her situation.

"Power outage?" The man sounded confused. "I did not receive any notice of such…"

"Perhaps you could look at the *Evening Standard* or BBC London. They both have coverage on the Holborn blackout."

"Hold on a sec. I'm checking now."

The music began again. It made her dizzy.

Joyce looked at her phone. It had twenty per cent battery remaining.

"Crikey!" the man quickly apologised. "Do forgive me, Miss Peng. I've just received an email informing us about a short circuit in the underground Holborn electrical system, so power and water are temporarily off. It's quite dangerous. Please don't attempt to go back to your flat for now."

Joyce almost laughed. If there were no electricity, the doors wouldn't open, and the lifts wouldn't work; she had no other way of getting back.

"How long should I wait?"

Silence at the other end, then David advised, "I'm sorry, I'm afraid this fire might last for hours. I would suggest you find alternative accommodation for tonight."

"Well," Joyce sighed.

"I've also received instructions that if our tenants at the Kean Street Apartments decide to stay at nearby hotels, NP Properties will reimburse your expenses later."

Joyce smiled upon hearing this but then remembered that her passport and driver's licence were still inside her apartment. She noticed the remaining battery on her phone. "I'd appreciate it if you contact me at once when you have more updates."

"Should we reach you at this number? It's not the one I have in my database here."

Joyce thought.

*It's Wednesday…three more days to go.*

"Yes," she confirmed. "Use this number for now. Thanks."

"Miss Peng, thank you for your understanding. We are sincerely sorry for any inconvenience."

After the call, Joyce stared at the clock on the cream wall. It had twelve species of birds to represent the hours. The hour hand pivoted to a robin and neared seven. She borrowed a charger from the owner. Sometime later, he told her that they would be closing soon.

Her battery had gone up to fifty per cent.

Leaving the Strand, Joyce wandered around and ended up in a Korean takeout. Luckily the place was far enough away from the fire and had a fully operating till.

She bought two cups of yuzu teas and sat at the counter, watching the street.

\* \* \*

Joyce collected her thoughts, picked up the ticket from *A View from the Bridge*, and put it back into her diary.

She recalled the performance from earlier. The ending where it had rained theatrical blood had been too much for her.

She flipped through her diary. Even if she couldn't go back to the flat today, there were no pressing matters tomorrow...nor the day after that... nor in the near future.

Putting her diary down, Joyce reached for the second tea.

*Now. Let us see where we shall spend the night.*

She looked out of the window as passers-by hurried home and coughed.

"Kke keke..."

She set down her tea and sought a pack of tissues from her blazer pocket. It was empty.

"If you don't mind, you can use mine." An old gentleman two seats away offered her a pale green napkin.

"Ahem. Thank you..." She took the napkin and coughed again.

"Are you alright?" the man asked with a concerned face. "I could help, although I am not sure if the Heimlich Manoeuvre would work for liquids."

"Thank you. I'm fine. I'm really fine." Joyce cleared her throat and sat upright. She smiled. "It's just...I've become homeless for the time being."

"Huh?" The man winced. "Are you a victim of the fire?"

"Spot on." Joyce picked up her used napkin and slipped it into an empty plastic teacup. "My agency said I had better find another place tonight."

"They told us the same thing. But my property manager said I should wait, hoping they would put out the fire tonight," the man responded, then had a spoonful of his beef bibimbap.

"I'm...not so sure." Joyce took out her phone, found her album, opened a video and showed it to the man. "I filmed this on Kingsway. There were at least ten fire engines."

The man moved closer and took her phone. Smoke and flames filled the screen.

"Perhaps I need to find a place to stay as well." He returned Joyce's phone, took out his phone, and made a call.

Joyce slumped in her seat and thought hard.

Where should she go? Where *could* she go?

Perhaps she could try Tilly? She shook her head and hesitated.

*A message won't hurt.*

She unlocked her phone, browsed through her contacts, found a name in her 'Favourites' and typed up a quick text.

*It's Joyce. I have a little emergency and was wondering if I could stay at your place tonight?*

She hoped that Tilly had not changed her number.

Her text was sent. Her head throbbed. And her heart sank.

"As we seem to be in the same boat, would you care to chat for a while?" the man inquired. "Are you travelling?"

Joyce tittered. "No. I live here."

"I thought you were either Japanese or Korean."

"Care to guess again?" She then added, "I'm Chinese."

"I've been to Macau," the man nodded. "Quite a nice place." He paused, not sure whether to continue. "How long have you been living in London?"

Joyce counted, "From boarding school to uni. Then I went back home for a few years."

"Ah. I should have known from your accent. Where did you study?"

Joyce laughed. "Just down the road. KCL."

"Well." The man laughed as well. "Care to guess where I studied my Master's?" He winked. "The same school."

"What did you study?"

"Mathematics, thirty years ago. What about you?"

"Sociology."

"When I was on my course, the school didn't even have the Waterloo Campus." The man shrugged. "It's quite different now. They have a new principal, and they are after Bush House."

Joyce sipped her drink with caution. "I heard they closed the shooting range – the one in the abandoned Underground station."

"I'm not sure I knew that." The man's eyes drifted to the entrance.

"Sorry, I'm late. Quite an evening rush."

A dark-haired man walked in. He had a black coat, a brown turtleneck and a Paul Smith scarf. He looked similar in age to the other man. "I just got your voicemail – a fire in Holborn. I thought you meant it as an April Fool's joke. Holborn and Kingsway are closed. I drove around from Tottenham Court Road," he said as he took off his scarf.

"I'm having a lovely chat with my alumna here." The man introduced Joyce and his friend. "This is my mate. The posh term, I believe, would be 'significant other'."

Joyce greeted the dark-haired man.

"It seems that I can't go back tonight. How would you feel if I stayed at your place?" the silver-haired man asked.

"Emergency lends itself to emergency measures." The dark-haired man sighed. "Allow me to grab a bite first. I didn't have lunch, and I have a rather annoying rumbly in my tumbly," he said as he walked to the counter.

"We live apart," the other man explained. "You know, trying to avoid co-living and all the botheration it brings. Some say it'll wear out love."

Joyce nodded. "Good that you have a place to stay now."

"What are your plans? Crashing at a friend's house?"

Joyce checked. There were no messages on her phone.

"I'm not sure yet. But I'll figure something out." She checked the time. "I guess I'll go now. Have a nice evening."

Joyce disposed of her trash, put on her shoulder bag, and stepped out onto the London streets once again.

Eight twenty.

Joyce headed to the Strand as she pondered her options.

If she received no reply from Tilly by twelve, she might as well rest on one of the benches in the basement of the King's Building.

She stopped at an intersection, startled by the unusual scene.

No traffic lights, no lamp posts, no annoying advertisements; a glowing collection of cars sped through the darkness, none willing to slow down.

Previously well-behaved drivers honked and rushed.

*Talk about the state of nature…*

Joyce crossed the road after a long wait and turned in the direction of Waterloo Bridge. She glanced back and thought it looked like a satellite image of a night scene of North Korea. She might as well find some cardboard and shelter under the bridge.

*An ethnography of the London homeless community…*

She continued to the middle of the bridge.

Or…

Joyce thought, *what if I dive?*

She held onto the railing with both hands, lowered her head, and stared at the water.

Then her phone buzzed.

She stood back. The stone pavement under her feet was somewhat reassuring.

Joyce took out her phone; there was a message from Tilly.

*I'm still at work. Maybe you can meet me at home? I'll be back about ten.*

Joyce skipped with delight.

She sent a quick reply and turned to the Strand once again.

It would take some time to get to Stratford by tube from here. Holborn was closed…Chancery Lane?

Joyce rechecked the time. Quarter to nine. She hadn't seen Tilly for a while. Perhaps she should bring something as a reconciliation gift. She decided to check out a store she had seen earlier.

\* \* \*

Stepping out of Gants Hill Station, Tilly Wurman felt uneasy.

Her wristwatch pointed to half-past nine. The bus stop across the street was empty. Perhaps she could catch the 179. Undecided, she stood still for a while. She usually preferred walking home after her evening shifts. The walk would take ten minutes, even for a slow walker like Tilly. Although the bus offered a quick lift, the waiting was killing.

Tilly decided to walk. She checked her Nokia once she'd got round the corner.

No new messages.

*Perhaps she had had second thoughts…or she had meant it as a joke…*

Tilly slung her bag over her shoulder and sauntered down Woodford Avenue. She wasn't even sure when Joyce had got back to London.

Swarms of insects gathered under soft streetlights. A cat silhouetted against the sidewalk, upon seeing her, dragged its tail and escaped into the recumbent shrubs. Some birds sang their nocturnal chorus in the nearby grass.

*It seemed spring was no longer far away from London.*

She smiled wryly.

She passed the Post Office and took a left turn on to a side road.

Orange light leaked from several houses. She could faintly hear some rock and roll playing and someone sneezing.

Tilly sighed.

Although she always welcomed springtime, Joyce was less partial to pollen and hay fever.

A flash of headlights cut through her thoughts, and she made way for the car.

*If she couldn't stay in her flat because of the fire, she could always go to a hotel or resort to her family in Mayfair.*

Tilly concluded that Joyce was not in such a dire situation that she needed to crash on her couch.

A dog barked in the distance, and a cat's scream pierced the night sky.

Tilly stopped in front of the off-licence and hesitated about going in. The cash she had brought should be enough to cover some extra food items. She did the mental math and pushed open the door.

Abdul, the shop owner, was watching *The Great British Bake Off*. He raised his hand in greeting. There were a few Twinkies stacked on the nearest shelf. Perhaps someone had ordered them. Tilly looked around and finally picked a hand of matured bananas, beef, ham, and some soft bread.

With her new purchases in a bag, Tilly continued her walk. Before she turned again, she saw a bouquet of white roses resting on a rubbish bin, the petals still fresh. She couldn't pinpoint someone around the neighbourhood who would waste something like this.

*Perhaps a broken heart.*

Tilly looked around but saw no one. She was tempted to save the flowers for her house. They could last a week or two.

She walked over and was just about to grab the flowers before remembering Joyce's visit and her allergies.

"Don't you dare leave the house, you little brat!" someone shouted behind her. It was her neighbour, Mr Oscar.

Tilly turned and saw the middle-aged man in his wrinkled shirt and cargo trousers, stomping under the streetlight. Then she heard the noises of a skateboard slashing against the tarred road.

Shawn was in trouble again.

"Hello, Tilly."

Her neighbour's son manoeuvred his skateboard to a halt in a backward turn. "Holborn's on fire? Wish it was our school."

Before she could say anything, the boy had gone.

The pharmacy where Tilly worked was close to Russell Square and had not been affected by the fire. Her colleague Zahren complained that if the pharmacy had been a little further south, they could have had paid leave and a nice break.

"Evening, Tilly. Oh, it's Mrs Wurman now, isn't it," Oscar greeted her with caution, standing in front of his mailbox. "I hope he didn't give you a fright."

He stroked his balding head. "How bad could it be? Pre-exam nerves? But it's still some time until May and June."

"It's hard to say." Tilly tilted her head. "I'd suggest trying not to put too much pressure on him." She paused. "When I did my GCSEs, I struggled with Physics – all the terms, laws, and formulae. They were overwhelming."

"Umm…" Oscar scratched his head in disappointment. "He's so careless. Look at 'im. Penny and I worked so hard for 'im to go to an independent, and he doesn't appreciate all our efforts. Now, right before exams, he wants to practise for a street competition. I hoped he could be more considerate. Like you, even."

Her neighbour let out a long breath and returned to the house. Tilly clutched her bag and stood in the same spot for a long time. Somehow, she knew Oscar's unfinished line – even an adopted child could behave better than Shawn.

*Even an ill, abandoned Chinese baby.*

\* \* \*

Walking up to the front door, Tilly looked at her watch.

Nine fifty-nine.

She'd lingered longer than she thought.

A shadowy figure huddled on her porch.

Joyce had come after all.

Tilly moved closer and gave her a gentle push. "Joy?"

"Wha!"

Joyce's eyes opened wide; her face frightened. She saw Tilly and gathered her senses. "Hi," she said. "It's been a while." She stood up, exercising her legs.

They hugged lightly.

"Your message…I was surprised…" Tilly broke the moment to retrieve her mail. "Saying that you'd be staying over."

"Sorry." Joyce combed her hair with her hand. "Long story…"

"I know." Tilly took out her key. "The Holborn fire, wasn't it?"

"Ah…" Joyce smiled bitterly, "you knew. Still at the same pharmacy?"

"Yep." Tilly opened the door. "Where else could I go? Though there are no Easter breaks, and you need two months' notice to apply for annual leave. But the pay's good and the shifts are okay. Can't complain."

"Pity that I wasn't invited to the wedding." Joyce seemed to have a ghastly pallor under the streetlight. "Nice ring."

"Thanks." Tilly touched the white gold band on her hand. "He's at a pharma company. Busy as well."

"If I'd known, I wouldn't have bothered you." Joyce hesitated outside the door.

"Don't be silly. He's away; a business trip to Bangalore. Testing new drugs."

"And Mr and Mrs Barcroft?"

"They moved back to Newcastle last year. You know, dad fancies John Turner and his notion of 'housing as a verb'. They liked it more there."

"No child yet?"

"No." Tilly hesitated and added, "Too much trouble for us."

They removed their shoes, changed into slippers and entered the living room. Faint traces of mould floated in the air.

"It's a bit chilly, isn't it? I'll turn on the heating." Tilly dropped off her bag, lanyard, and mail on a round wooden table.

"Tilly Wurman…" Joyce leaned over and peeked.

"You haven't eaten, have you?" Tilly squeezed a smile. "Hold on. I'll go make some sandwiches."

"Right-oh." Joyce put her bag down and pulled out a bottle of champagne wrapped in golden packaging. "Belated wedding gift. Hope you don't mind."

Tilly read the label: Louis Roederer Brut Vintage 2003.

"When Mr Wurman returns from his trip, you can celebrate together," Joyce said as she settled on the sofa.

"I wish you hadn't," Tilly grumbled. "I discovered a white wine from

Tesco last year. It was only four quid but tasted better than any white wine I've ever had. I have one here. Maybe we can try it."

"Sounds good." Joyce stood up. "Mind if I use your bathroom? I drank so much water before coming here, and I almost borrowed your backyard."

"Go ahead," Tilly nodded. "You remember the way? Upstairs on the right-hand side. The light is on the left; be careful not to slip."

Dinner was simple: olives, ham and spinach sandwiches, and bananas with yoghurt.

"Not bad, is it?" Tilly asked as Joyce sipped the white wine. "At least it doesn't taste any worse than the fancy brands."

Joyce pondered. "Not bad at all. A blend, eh? They say some blends are so good that even the best sommeliers can't tell."

"When'd you get back?" Tilly asked as she chewed an olive.

"Recently." Joyce put down her glass and leaned back on the sofa. She twiddled the tassels on the tablecloth. "Last Friday."

"Bad timing."

Joyce laughed. "The flat's not in a great state, either. Dust jammed the bathroom fan. I found some mysterious substance behind the sofa that resembled mouse shit and some mummified insect carcasses. I hired a cleaner for next Monday."

"Hope the fire will be out by then." Tilly removed the plates. "Quite difficult if you can't go in."

"Counting on that." Joyce reached for her diary. "Or if circumstances ran against my favour, I would need to contact the cleaning service." She found the page titled 6th April. "The appointment is at nine in the morning. I guess I can wait until Sunday late afternoon."

Joyce closed her diary and sighed. "I had an encounter today that made me feel that the London crowd was unfriendly. I went to a play earlier and thought I'd have some gummies before the show started. An old lady beside me complained to the usher that I didn't know the rules." She ground her teeth. "The worst part, though, was that she kept coughing during the play."

Tilly ignored her complaints. "I'll go upstairs and arrange the guest room. Do you need another nightcap? A glass of port, maybe?"

"I'm good for now." Joyce stood up and arranged the chairs. "There's no need to sort out the guest room. I can use the couch. And could I borrow a phone charger?"

"Apple?"

"Yes."

"Well, I only have my Nokia one. I'll need to look for one."

Tilly went upstairs to the storage room and turned on the light. Clouds of dust were suspended in mid-air. "Let's see." She pulled out a storage box from the top shelf. The handle, which was superglued onto the box, had a label that read 'ELECTRONICS'. Tilly rummaged through its contents and finally found an iPhone charger.

She headed downstairs and showed Joyce the charger. "Is this okay?"

Joyce looked then shook her head. "It's for older models."

"In that case, I can go to the Apple Store in Covent Garden tomorrow during my lunch break."

"I was hoping to contact my property manager." Joyce stretched her legs. "Can I borrow your laptop to send a quick email?"

Tilly was about to say that her old HP was out at a service centre before remembering that Martin still had an old MacBook from his student years; she'd just seen it. "I'll go and get it."

Tilly brought down the laptop, which was as heavy as an anatomy dictionary, together with its power leads.

"One might as well call this an artefact," Joyce commented. "This is the first time I've ever seen an Apple iBook."

Tilly felt reassured. Martin had always spoken highly of his computer, citing it as the archetype for all MacBooks. She set the device and assorted accessories down on the sofa. "It's the only working laptop I have at home. It doesn't have a built-in battery, so you have to use the leads. Be careful not to trip over." She paused. "I have an early morning. Would you like a shower?"

Joyce nodded. "Yes."

"I'll get you a blanket and some towels." Tilly walked into the kitchen. "The shower has been acting up lately. It gives you cold water once the hot water starts running and takes about twenty seconds to sort itself out. Just let it run and wait. There are new toothbrushes and floss behind the mirror."

"Got it." Joyce's voice faded away as she climbed the stairs.

Tilly opened her dryer and took out a large and a small towel. She turned off the kitchen light and found her way to the bathroom, knocking softly on the door.

"I've put the towels by the door, okay?"

Question asked, but no reply offered.

Tilly heard running water and clattering through the frosted glass.

"Joy? Everything alright? I'm coming in."

She opened the door slowly and was taken aback by the scene – Joyce was hugging the toilet, vomiting.

"Too much wine?" Tilly joked as she put down the towels and patted Joyce on her back. "You used to have a higher threshold."

Joyce shifted her body before another gush. The sounds and smell made Tilly nearly nauseous as well.

She watched as Joyce twisted and took off a wig.

"Wha...wait..."

Tilly didn't know what to say.

"You know, chemotherapy is a great way of saving money at the hairdresser's," Joyce joked as she set her wig aside and slipped behind the shower curtain.

"I...I'll get the guest room ready."

Tilly excused herself and made to leave.

She tried to grasp the situation. She looked at her watch. Five past midnight. It didn't seem like an April Fool's joke.

*Later.*

Tilly waited for Joyce to finish her shower and then helped her into the guest room.

"No need to treat me like a patient, please. My mind might be falling behind, but my limbs are still good to go." Joyce dropped her slippers and sat down on the bed.

"A brain problem, then."

"Nothing that I can't handle. I've got meningioma, a benign one." Joyce smiled faintly. "I had an operation in Shanghai. I'm a lot better now – only minor migraines. The tricky part is that I left my steroids at the apartment. Honestly, who would have thought that a fire could break out in Holborn? So here I am, without my phone charger, without my medication." Joyce leaned back. "Say, if my migraine gets a little... uncooperative, can I borrow something?" Her eyes drifted to the bedside table. There was a rolled-up blue necktie on it.

Tilly pocketed the necktie. "No more alcohol." She regretted their earlier wine tasting session now.

"Nothing of the sort."

"And nothing harmful to your condition." Tilly's tone hardened.

Joyce shot up like an unfolded pocketknife. "Wait here."

With that, she plodded out of the room barefooted.

Tilly lowered her head into her hands; it had been such a long evening.

"Can I have some of these?"

Tilly looked up. Joyce leaned against the doorframe, holding something in her hand. Three boxes of codeine tablets. Their blue packaging appeared green under the faint light. Tilly had kept them after Martin had recovered from a leg fracture last year.

"Don't be silly," she sighed. "I know a few places where you can walk in without an appointment. I recommend a clinic in Soho. The doctors there could prescribe you something more appropriate."

Joyce got closer and said something that threw Tilly off balance.

"Have you ever thought about suicide? I've heard that codeine works."

\* \* \*

The next day, Tilly got up, went through her morning routine, and headed downstairs.

Joyce was resting on the sofa, wrapped in a blanket, a pen in her hand, writing in her diary.

"G' morning."

"Morning." Joyce looked up. "Sleep well?"

"Not bad," Tilly lied.

She had spent a few hours last night thinking, and thinking didn't get her anywhere.

It was six-fifty – time to get ready for work.

"Want some coffee?" Tilly went to the kitchen, opened the fridge, and took out some bread, a bottle of milk, and leftovers from their late dinner.

"Milk would do." Joyce put her slippers on and made her way to the kitchen.

Tilly noticed that Joyce's wig, although convincing, at first sight, looked less natural close up.

"A…choo!" Joyce sneezed a few times.

"Bless you." Tilly assembled her breakfast. "Now that spring is close, another season for you to suffer."

"Can't say that I enjoy spring." Joyce grabbed some tissues and wiped her nose. "Trying more culinary pursuits?" She pointed to a row of neatly arranged homemade pickles on the countertop.

"Courtesy of Martin," Tilly laughed. "I'm still stuck with curry. The only dish that I'm good at."

Joyce picked up a jar of sundried tomatoes. "A signature dish beats an assortment of so-so ones. No one can never get enough of your curry."

Tilly felt uneasy again. She put a glass beside the milk and bread. "Hot or cold?"

"Leave it to me." Joyce twisted open the milk bottle and poured half a glass. "I'm sorry that I…came to visit last night."

"You can stay until the flat's all sorted." Tilly brought the kettle to a boil.

Joyce drank her milk. "Thanks." She spoke as a half-circle of milk painted her mouth like a white beard.

They left for the station together.

*Later.*

Tilly had her lunch at a sandwich shop near the pharmacy. After, she wandered and ended up at a curry house. Lunchtime always paid well for the owner there. A line queued to the door and beyond. Tilly did not place an order. She spent some time in its washroom.

One of the spotlights inside didn't function well, and the other was broken. The malfunctioning one shone like an anglerfish in the dark.

Tilly rubbed the bags under her eyes. Her fingers were cold, bringing comfort to her eyes.

She remembered Joyce's question.

*'Have you ever thought about suicide? I've heard that codeine works.'*

She had been too shocked to answer, and things spiralled out of control as she pulled herself together.

Joyce had tried to kiss her. She didn't let her.

One step forward and two steps back.

Tilly knew that they could no longer be best friends once they had stepped away from each other.

She massaged her stiff calves from standing all morning.

*I should have ignored her message.*

Tilly rubbed her hands and face and let out a sigh. She was not a good liar: not to herself and not to others.

"Will you please hurry up?" Someone was knocking on the door urgently.

"Coming."

Tilly looked at her watch. Her lunch break was about to end.

She flushed the toilet and opened the door.

Time to face the music playing in her pharmacy again.

\* \* \*

Drizzle tainted Tilly's way back home.

Early signs of spring had retreated into harsh coldness while raindrops tap-danced on her umbrella.

The white roses were still on the bin; their petals had withered in the wind.

Tilly could not help but think about Joyce's question about suicide.

*What if she actually had a malignant tumour?*

*What if the fire had given her a perfect excuse to pay the last visit?*

*What if...*

Tilly had learnt at a young age that what-ifs were the most difficult questions to answer.

What if she had never been adopted? What if she had never had her operation? What if she had never met Joyce?

What-ifs rarely worked well with her.

Tilly shuddered. She dared not go down this path.

With her keys in her hand, she made a mental note to talk to Joyce later, to make sure she had no...problems.

She wondered when she would be back or if she would be back at all.

"Back so early?" A voice from the kitchen startled her.

Tilly dropped her keys. She rushed into the kitchen. Joyce was drinking tea.

"I used some of your cardamoms." Joyce handed her a white mug.

Tilly hesitated, then finally took it.

"I've borrowed your spare key as well. We all make a habit of keeping them under doormats." Her visitor smiled once again. "I went to get a charger and forgot that I'd asked you for a spare. I hope that you don't mind."

Joyce sat down. "They're still struggling with the fire. I heard the most dreadful thing today. It seems a group of robbers plotted the fire so they could break into a vault at Hatton Garden. The fire took many CCTVs down."

Tilly took off her flats and changed into her slippers. "Someone at work saw them using loaders to dig up the ground. Not the robbers, the firefighters. I also heard that many restaurants in Covent Garden suffered from a power outage, and they have no way of maintaining their expensive raw ingredients. Terrible losses."

Tilly retreated to her living room and was left speechless. Three boxes of codeine tablets rested on the table. She had hidden them in the kitchen before she went to work this morning.

"What tricks are you trying to pull?" Tilly lost control and shouted at Joyce. "This is no joke!"

"Someone once said that codeine and alcohol are a great combo for suicide. Do you know who said it?"

"NO! AND I DON'T WANT TO KNOW! Just stop trying my nerves for once!"

Tilly kicked a table leg, and the boxes of tablets jerked.

"James Bond."

Joyce sipped her milk tea then laughed. "Silly Tilly, worrying about me? That's very kind of you, but I wasn't thinking of killing myself. Not yet."

"Then what's all this for? A show?" Tilly almost cried.

"I'm writing a novel." Joyce picked up a box of codeine tablets. "The protagonist's best friend has committed suicide, and she is reconciling with her loss on her way to the funeral." She opened the box and peeked inside. "I used to love reading Durkheim's *Suicide*. Since I got sick, I have changed my mind on many things. Well, my mind did change, didn't it?"

Joyce spoke slowly. "Now I wanted to cross one item off my bucket list and finally start writing something." She yawned. "I ran some searches online. Can you believe that there are websites that teach people how to commit suicide? One of the suggestions was codeine. Well, since I'm not the pharmacist here, perhaps you could lend me your expertise on this matter?"

"Not sure if I can help." Tilly smiled sadly.

"My source of information says that the lethal dosage would be 2.4 grams." Joyce turned the box over. "This says each pill contains 3 milligrams, so you'd need 800 tablets. Not an efficient method, is it?" She put the box down. "There are around 70 pills here. Say if someone swallows them in one go, what are the odds they survive?"

"That'll depend on whether the person has a tolerance or not," Tilly pondered. "Let's say the effect varies from person to person. And there is a difference if the person has a full stomach or not." Tilly picked up her cup of tea and stood closer. "I'm only answering your questions because you want to research for your story. All I can say is that if codeine and aspirin were taken together, the result would be more...deadly."

Sitting down, Joyce tilted her chin and thought. "I've read that alcohol intake can speed up the process. However, another way of losing consciousness was mentioned. Use a plastic bag to cover your nose and mouth and secure it with a rubber band."

Tilly rubbed her temples. "All this dangerous content; it shouldn't be online."

"There is someone who wrote books on this subject matter," Joyce recalled. "Derek Humphrey. There is a 'right to die' philosophy."

Tilly shook her head. "But life is the most...how can they..." she trailed off.

Joyce opened her mouth as if to retort but fell silent. After a while, she said, "There is a need to be prepared. Like a midwife preparing for a new-born. Well, let's get back to my story."

"Speaking of which…" Tilly smiled. "It should be 'aspirin and wine', not 'codeine and alcohol'. Make no mistake."

Joyce laughed like a horse. "I'll remember now for sure. Do you remember that when I told you that Bond is known as agent 'double-zero-seven' elsewhere, you made such a face? You said it sounded like a reference number for ordering farm equipment."

"Fleming specified in his book that Bond is one of the rare 'double-O' agents. How can they call him 'double-zero'?"

"It's the same with the French." Joyce knitted her brows. "Interesting why there was such a difference. Perhaps it is that 'o' and '0' look so similar that they mixed it up in the translation."

The doorbell rang.

Joyce stood and stretched. "Clear the table, will you? It looks like my Domino's has arrived on time."

# CHAPTER 2

Another day went by like water under a bridge. Nothing turbulent happened, except that Joyce mistook some of Martin's pickled peppers for cherry tomatoes.

They had the same breakfast: milk, stale bread, and bananas.

Dinner was delivered again.

When Tilly got home from work, she chatted a while with Joyce about her book. Then they bid good night to each other, one crouched on the sofa, another stretched in bed.

On the third morning, Joyce finally heard back from her property manager. Although there were intermittent supplies of utilities, the fire had been put out. She could go back to her flat.

The pair did not hug before parting; instead, they smiled at each other.

"Thank you for allowing me to stay." Joyce bent down and tied her shoelaces. "And don't worry, I'll acknowledge you in my book. If I ever finish it. When Martin comes back from his trip, shall we have dinner together?"

Tilly nodded. "Take care, gal. Follow doctor's orders and no more drinking. Professional advice from an old friend."

Joyce bit her lip as if wanting to say something but just smirked. "This is not goodbye. I'm sure we'll see each other again soon." She opened the door and went out.

Tilly continued with her preparations for work.

She left the house at seven o'clock sharp. As she passed a refuse loader, she saw the remains of the white rose bouquet disappearing into a light Friday morning mist.

She arrived at Gants Hill in a trance and got on the Central Line towards Holborn.

The morning rushers carried a certain heaviness, staring blankly at their respective phones, watches, papers, and fingers.

Tilly steadied herself by gripping onto a handle. Someone beside her showed a sweat-stained armpit, and the smell made her want to get off at the next stop.

She saw her weariness in the reflection of the window and wondered if she had become a member of the nine-to-five urban zombie gang.

The stench seemed to grow every second.

Tilly turned her head and cast her eyes elsewhere.

She had a vague feeling that something was going to go wrong. Be it a failed exam, a breakup, a miscalculation, or a car accident that left Martin bed-bound for weeks, and she could always sense forebodings.

What would happen this time?

\* \* \*

Turning into Kean Street, Joyce meandered back home with her bag on her back and a large hot chocolate from Caffè Nero in her hand. A few smokers were standing in front of the office building on her right.

"One hundred and fifty firefighters were called to the scene and twenty-five fire engines...with an economic loss estimated to be over one million..."

came the voice of a news announcer in her wireless headphones. She sighed as her eyes took in rows of large portable generators lined up like coffins on both sides of the road.

A helicopter hovered above her. She took off her headphones and looked up.

The helicopter flew south, and she returned to her walk. After a few steps, she felt her phone vibrating in her blazer's pocket.

It was her brother Jayden calling.

*How did he get my new number?*

She hesitated before answering.

"Do me a good favour! Next time, before you vanish, say something! Leave a note, message me, write something on your blast mirror! You have no idea how worried we've been about you. We were almost on our way to the police to report a missing person!"

As soon as the call connected, Joyce felt she had made a mistake.

"No need to shout. I'm your sister, not one of your subordinates. There's no need for me to file a report before I do anything. I'm an adult, after all."

"And I'm your brother, not your dog. I don't have all day to trace your whereabouts," Jayden said. "Back to London so quickly? I can fly out on Tuesday. Let's have dinner and talk. Talk for real."

"Hello? Hello?" Joyce pretended. "The signal is weak. Ahh! I should never have switched! Call you later." She hung up and pocketed her phone.

"Pretty woman. I've been cheated by you…"

She hummed one of her makeshift songs and stepped into the apartment lobby. All she wanted was a nice, long bath before thinking about anything else. She took out her key card but then stopped.

A man was slumping against the wall by the mailboxes. He had a tattered, brown jacket, a haggard face, and unkempt hair. Had a homeless man found his way in here?

"You alright?" Joyce walked up. "Look, here, I've a hot chocolate. I haven't touched it. Would you like it?" She crouched down and handed the foam cup to the man.

His stubble moved like a rabbit's mouth before he spoke. "Much appreciated. This could really help." He took the drink and stared at Joyce. "I'm David from NP Properties. Are you…Miss Peng?"

"Yes."

The man stood up, excited, and almost knocked over the hot chocolate. "We spoke earlier. Thank God you're back at last. I've been waiting for you."

"For me?" Joyce was puzzled. "Is there another problem with the flat?"

"No, no, no. Please don't worry. The fire is out, and for good, one might say. In response to the inconvenience this fire has caused you, I want to apologise on behalf of the company." He lowered his head. "And because of the power outage, our access control and CCTV systems have not been restored yet. We don't expect them to be restored until next Wednesday. The utilities are theoretically running, but, as you may have noticed, the area has been dug up quite badly, so if there is a gas leak, please call our emergency services."

David took out a Post-it from his jacket pocket. "Please call this number if you have any problems with the flat."

"Sure. Thank you." Joyce took the note and looked at the man in front of her. "You look like you haven't slept in days. Why don't you come upstairs and get some rest?"

"That's very kind of you." David was flattered and waved his hand eagerly. "It's nothing." He gulped the hot chocolate. "The past three days, I've been busy leading the way for the firefighters. With the power out, we couldn't

use any of the lifts, so we had to climb the stairs several times every hour."
He smiled faintly. "A rather good workout, I have to say. Which is why
I'm giving up the idea of participating in this year's Gherkin Challenge."

He laughed bitterly, then looked at his watch. "I need to get back to the
office. I have given Mr Peng a report on the situation."

*I see.* Joyce smiled.

He bid her goodbye. Joyce went back to her apartment, had a nice bubble
bath, dried her hair and got into bed.

When she woke up, it was four forty-three in the afternoon.

Joyce walked downstairs to the kitchen. Boxes and jars of pills waited
for her on the mahogany kitchen table. She took a few pills and swallowed
them dry.

Dressed, with sunglasses on, phone fully charged, and keys in hand, Joyce
took the lift to go downstairs.

The lobby was deserted like an alien planet. She found her mailbox and
opened it. Three ads from other estate agents asked if she wanted to sell the
apartment. Joyce slipped the ads into a neighbour's mailbox on her way out.

At five p.m., the restaurant on the corner of Drury Lane was already
hosting many diners. Candlelight shone on silver cutlery, and laughter
mingled with wine glasses clinking.

Joyce peered into the restaurant's window. The people inside seemed to
have forgotten that a fire had broken out nearby that had startled London
only three days ago. Perhaps the diners had shared the usual topics: stocks
buybacks, horses, slideware, and the weather.

She walked on.

The theatres were finally back in business.

She turned the corner to catch the end of the afternoon session at the

Aldwych Theatre. The audience had spilt onto the roadside like dispersed spiderlings hatching, each holding a programme for the *Carole King Musical*. A double-decker bus manoeuvred itself slowly, like a stranded whale trying to get back to the water.

Joyce felt like a dog trapped in a flock of ducks. She squeezed through the ruck and broke free.

The Duchess Theatre was showing *The Play That Goes Wrong*. She turned right onto Wellington Street then Bow Street. The sun lingered on the buildings to make a sand painting. The outer walls of the Royal Opera House were albicant with one indented part showing a giant plastic sphere with a ballerina inside. A man cranked his neck under the installation, looking at her dress.

Joyce stopped at Cicchetti. Its window was decorated with assortments of prosciutto, mussels, and fruits on crushed ice.

She removed her sunglasses, opened the door, and walked in.

"Good afternoon. Do you have a place for one? I don't have a reservation."

A waiter nodded lightly. "Of course. This way, please." He picked up a menu on the way and led her deeper into the restaurant.

Joyce smiled inwardly. The best thing about being alone was that even if you didn't have a reservation, the staff at most restaurants would find you a place. While the choice was often limited to dimly lit areas or corners, a table was a table.

"Please." The waiter set down the menu on the marble top and motioned a junior waiter to pull out a chair for Joyce.

As she had expected, they had placed her in a corner, facing the mirror on the wall.

"I'd rather sit on the other side." She looked at herself in the mirror and sat down on the sofa.

"Can I get you anything to drink?"

"I'd like a glass of wine, anything you could recommend."

"Sure."

After the waiter had left, Joyce picked up the menu and browsed casually. She looked at the empty seat across the table for two, remembering her first date with Tilly here. That had been in April too. Tilly had decided to sit on the couch with the mirror behind her. Joyce had always disliked mirrors. They reminded her of her mother, who had died young.

And Tilly?

She hadn't asked.

Her phone vibrated – a message from Jayden.

*Let's meet for dinner at Hakkasan. If you disappear again, I'll make sure to hunt you down.*

Joyce muted her phone.

"Excuse me. Have you decided yet?" a waiter asked.

She ordered tuna tartare and lasagne. The waiter confirmed her order and left.

A group of diners rushed in.

Suddenly, Joyce was glad that she had a corner seat. She would like some quietness over this dinner.

\* \* \*

Joyce didn't opt for the restaurant's dessert; she went to Ladurée in Covent Garden instead. The patisserie was quite crowded, with many people queuing for macaroon gift boxes. She walked up to the open terrace on the second floor, ordered a sorbet with rose petals and finished it in a corner. Then, she took a stroll through the shops in the Market. Friday evenings in Covent Garden were lively.

Joyce wandered from east to west before realising it was already seven o'clock. She watched a street magician performing in front of the Apple Store, contributed a tenner and left.

The darkness grew to match her loneliness.

Passing by the Aldwych Theatre again, she went to the ticket window on a whim and asked if there were any seats left for the show that night. She managed to secure a seat in the dress circle.

The musical ended sharply at ten. Joyce hummed the tune of 'Will You Still Love Me Tomorrow' in the lift back to the apartment.

A bird dashed out of the two rows of large terracotta flowerpots and headed for the moon.

These plants hadn't been there when she moved out three years ago. It seemed that her unmet new neighbour had green fingers.

She took her key and entered the penthouse. The curtains remained undrawn, and she could see the BT Tower in the distance.

She took off her shoes, walked barefoot upstairs, turned on a sidelight, and settled in a ladybug-themed bean bag – a birthday gift from Tilly.

*Better to change this train of thought.* She moved her shoulders, then picked up her MacBook and placed it on her knees.

She opened a new document, typed a sentence, and moved her finger to print it.

A display window appeared.

*Unable to Print.*

Joyce slid away from the bean bag, walked into her study, and found an unopened pack of A4 paper from Ryman's.

She tore open the package and bent down to remove the paper tray.

The tray had a stack of aged paper inside.

Joyce added another stack and tried again.

The yellow warning light on the screen was still flashing. She checked the wireless connection and knocked on the machine several times. Finally, it started to hum.

She stood up and found a small cut on her right index finger.

Perhaps it was not her lucky day after all.

The printer hummed again and entered its sleep mode.

If waiting was what it took to solve any of her problems, she might as well wait.

But reality didn't work like that. Life never worked like that.

She went down to the living room, slipped into a beige shawl, and went onto the balcony. Its black balustrade was spotted with guano. The night had dropped. The cold made her shiver. She wrapped the shawl tightly around her shoulders and leaned against the metal railing.

She thought about the times they had had here.

Drunk, kissing, flipping over the railing to sing and shout until the passers-by on the street started throwing shoes at them.

Joyce took a breath.

She suddenly wanted a cigarette, but she didn't want to go out again to get one.

Another helicopter crossed the sky. She wasn't sure if it was the same one she had seen this afternoon.

Joyce backed into the house. The night scene in Covent Garden shone as always, even brighter after the fire, and she knew something had changed.

She had changed.

She was no longer afraid. Not afraid of death or of living.

Her stomach gurgled.

*It'd be nice to have some curry now.* She thought as she drew the curtains.

\* \* \*

Sunday, 5th April.

Noon.

"Excuse me, are you Miss Joyce Peng?"

She had just entered the lift when someone called behind her. She put on her sunglasses.

"Yes. How can I help you?" Her voice was hoarse.

The woman took out a folder from her business case. "My name is Enid Abara; I'm with NP Properties. I'm just doing a routine check of our apartments at Kean Street. Do you mind if I ask you some questions?"

"Please make them quick."

Enid pulled out a questionnaire and started with the questions on the utilities. She managed to finish them in under two minutes.

"That'll be all," Enid said as she stored her pen. "Oh, sorry. My colleague David asked me to re-confirm your contact details. He said you had changed your phone number. Would you like us to put the new number in our database still?"

"Yes, please do that," she sniffed. "Sorry, it's the…hay fever." She smiled apologetically. "Springtime."

Enid took out a Kleenex and handed it to her. "My sister-in-law lives in Japan, and she suffers terribly from the pollen there. She needs to wear a mask on her way to and from work."

"Actually, I do have one." She reached into her blazer pocket and took out a mask. "Perhaps I'll use it once I'm outside."

Enid called up the lift again, and they entered together.

"Who would have thought of the fire?" Enid pressed the button for the ground floor. "And the CCTV's down. The road's dug up. I've walked all around the area to get here."

"Yes. Who would have thought of the fire?" Her client concurred with her.

"And the weather, it's quite cold. Some offices still don't have central air-conditioning restored."

"Oh?" Her client thought for a while and added, "But today does seem to be a good day for some curry." The lift doors opened, and she walked out first.

She didn't even say goodbye.

\* \* \*

Monday, 6th April.

Sarnai had not been doing too well lately.

*Well*, she thought. *The word 'too' was unnecessary.*

Yesterday, her husband had hinted at divorce.

Like many of her former employers, she knew that his words were intended to inform rather than negotiate.

Her bus was on time.

She folded her paper with care. There was another exclusive story about the Hatton Garden robbery. The article suggested that the burglars had something to do with the Holborn fire. Sarnai's grandmother had always told her to watch out for people who take advantage of a bad situation.

A bad situation. That was what she had got herself into now.

Didn't she work from early in the morning till late at night to provide for her daughter and her family?

She could have stood it, if he had only messed around, but then he started seeing the waitress from the bar downstairs.

When she came to the country, her husband had disliked her for her poor English. By the time she had learnt the language, he had still disliked her.

The bus door opened, and she folded her papers, put on her scarf and stepped out.

She would keep the papers, scrunch them into balls, and place them under her laundry when she got back, so her clothes would dry quicker.

Drizzle tainted Waterloo Bridge and her feelings.

Sarnai was beginning to hate London.

Maybe she had disliked London from an early age. It rained endlessly, and her life without a dryer had taught her that clothes wouldn't dry on the terrace for days.

The summers were lovely, she had to admit, but good weather was like a fleeting golden eagle: marvellous yet rare.

Sarnai sighed.

Those dunes and the flocks of sheep drifting under the cloudless sky... She could only visit them in her dreams now.

She followed the commuting crowd off the bridge and crossed the road after running a red light.

Sarnai hadn't been able to break the news to her daughter.

*Not yet.*

Her grandmother had another saying: 'you can find gold everywhere, but not parents'.

That was why she had stayed in Mongolia to take care of her husband's parents. That was why she didn't want to leave her seven-year-old daughter.

*Wants and needs are quite different things.*

Perhaps it was better for her to think forward. Where could she go? Back to Mongolia? Or visit her friend in Sussex first?

A divorce.

At least she had the freedom to have a divorce.

She almost missed her turn onto Kean Street.

*When had divorce sounded so much like a luxury?*

Perhaps she could make it work with her daughter. Nothing would stop her. She would scrub more floors and more toilets. No one would despise her for working hard.

Sarnai pulled back her thoughts. She had found the entrance to the apartments. The double glass door was open, saving her the trouble of digging out the key card.

Before entering the lift, Sarnai looked at her watch. Eight fifty-five. She was on time.

Now that her marriage was ruined, she couldn't lose this job.

She pressed the button for the ninth floor, took off her scarf, and took a deep breath.

The lift smelled okay. Not elegantly Mayfair-ish, not professionally Canary Wharf-ish.

She got out of the lift, turned right, opened the hallway door and entered the atrium.

Mrs Robinson's plants looked healthy enough.

*Maybe I can water the tomatoes later*, Sarnai thought as she stood in front of apartment five and rang the bell. Her feet trod comfortably on a doormat featuring the Union Flag.

"Good morning. Your cleaner is here." She knocked on the door.

No response.

She sighed. She could wait a bit and try to sort out some of her own issues.

The owner had only scheduled a three-hour spot. But it could be a trial, a test for an extended contract.

She leaned against a stone pillar. She had hoped that her husband was working and not slobbering.

He had brought home a tiny salary last year...

She should have known.

Five past nine.

Sarnai knocked on the door again.

Still no response. Perhaps there was no one at home. She felt relieved. If she were unable to enter by nine-thirty, she would still be compensated.

"Your cleaner has arrived. Miss...Peng?"

She glanced at her hand. Her employer for the day's details was written on the back of her hand.

No answer.

She knocked again.

"I'm sorry. What are you doing?"

A female voice.

Sarnai turned. An Asian woman appeared in front of her. She had a bulging shoulder bag and a stern expression.

"I...I..." Sarnai stammered. "I'm the cleaner. I have an appointment at nine." She showed the woman her hand.

"Right. That's what she told me." The woman stared at the apartment door for a while.

"Is she not in?"

"No. I'm afraid not, Miss. I mean Mrs." Sarnai noticed the other woman's ring.

"Joy? Joyce? Open up! It's me, Tilly. Open up!"

The woman rang the bell and pounded on the door.

"I've been waiting for a while, but I don't think she's home."

"Move over!" The woman stooped down and lifted a corner of the Union Flag doormat.

Sarnai stepped aside.

"She probably keeps a spare key somewhere." The woman fumbled on her knees, showing an edge of her pink underwear. "Here! Found it!" She got up and hurriedly inserted the key into the lock.

"Uhh…I'm not sure we should be doing this, Mrs Tilly," Sarnai hesitated. "I don't want to get into trouble."

"It's fine. We're good friends. I'll make sure nothing happens to you." The woman was agitated. "I just need to make sure…to check something very quickly."

She pushed the door open and went in.

Sarnai followed.

Later on, she would wish that she hadn't.

It was sweltering hot inside.

Sarnai took in the view in front of her. This maisonette had the same layout as the Robinsons'. Large blankets covered most of the furniture in the living room. Wine stains marked the fluffy cream carpet in the centre.

The air was stale and smelled like rotten bananas. Sarnai suspected that dust had clogged the ventilation system. The corners of the wall hosted traces of cobwebs. The stainless-steel sink in the Italian-designed island kitchen had a crust of limescale. A half-full Brita sat on the counter. The kitchen bin had no bag inside. A discarded takeaway package from a franchise curry chain stood beside it, with an empty wine bottle.

*This place needs a good cleaning. A spot won't do.*

Sarnai's eyes roamed around the room. A few bottles and boxes of medicine rested on the kitchen table together with an HSBC contactless bank card. Pills were scattered around like M&Ms. The woman paled upon seeing them.

"Joyce! Are you in!?" she shouted as she raced upstairs.

Sarnai followed.

The second-floor bedroom had closed curtains. In the dim light, she could see the outline of someone lying on the bed.

*A hangover…*

She had seen enough of her husband's idling in the daytime to draw her own conclusions.

"No! Joyce!" The woman turned on the light and let out a cry.

Sarnai set her eyes on the strangest sight she had ever seen.

A recumbent form on the bed.

A person.

The person had a black plastic bag on her head. The type that Sarnai often used in her line of work to take out refuse. Next to the bag, she was certain it was a wig and a cell phone.

*Could it be an unusual fetish?*

Sarnai had seen and heard enough odd tales in her work, yet nothing had prepared her for this sight.

Her feet would not move.

"Call the ambulance!" the woman shouted, throwing herself at the bedside. She untied the plastic bag; a stream of muddy liquid came out of the person's mouth.

"Y…yes…" Sarnai hurriedly pulled out her cell phone and pressed 103. The call didn't connect.

*Why so stupid! It should be 999. This is London, not Ulaanbaatar!*

She dialled again as the woman busied herself with first-aid procedures. "Your call has been…"

"Give it to me!" the woman ordered.

Seeing her red-rimmed eyes, Sarnai knew better to comply than to ask. The woman dropped onto the floor as if all her energy had been sapped away. "Please…tell the front desk…we have a situation."

Sarnai nodded and escaped quickly. She remembered the horoscope column she had read earlier on the bus. It said that she would have a turning point in her life.

*How accurate it was.*

Now she no longer wanted to keep her job.

\* \* \*

Catherine Roxborough breathed a sigh of relief.

*Home sweet home!*

Putting her keys away, she set down her luggage and pet carrier as she greeted the empty house. A little dust had gathered on the floor. The rest of the house was as good as she had left it a year ago.

Catherine had left on a whim, and her best friend Mick had not burrowed into the reason. She was grateful for that. She needed a little time and peace for herself. Mick had even agreed to take in Mr Darcy during her time away. Now that his wedding was approaching, she would hunt down the best of worldly goods as a sign of her appreciation.

"Come on, Mr Darcy. Don't be shy. It's good to be home, isn't it?"

Catherine bent down to open the pet carrier. A striped ginger cat moved out as if he were a geologist exploring an underground cave. His whiskers shivered cautiously.

"Why don't we have a little kip upstairs first?" she suggested as she picked up the cat.

The flight from New Delhi to London had taken nearly ten hours, and she was exhausted.

*Unpacking could wait.*

Catherine changed into her baffies and headed upstairs to the bedroom.

The landline rang. She checked the caller's number but didn't answer.

Moments later, her pre-recorded reply began to play. "Hello! This is Catherine and Pierre's home. We are out of town. Leave a message…and, if you're looking for Mr Darcy, leave a message, and we promise we won't call back!"

*Pierre…*

Her heart sank at the mention of his name. And the joke on Mr Darcy no longer made her laugh.

"Cathy," came her uncle's steady voice. "I know you're back. Call me later."

The message ended.

She hugged and kissed her cat, feeling better.

The phone rang again. She peeked. It was her Uncle Alexander again.

"Um…perhaps you should consider changing your answering machine message."

The message ended with a beep, and Catherine no longer wanted to rest.

Catherine struggled but managed to open her overpacked suitcases. A small, wooden figure flew out of the compartments, and she was quick enough to catch it mid-air. The little sculpture was a farewell present from the school, where she had volunteered to teach English for a year.

Catherine got up and placed the figure on a side desk. Then she removed a large collection of dirty laundry, a paperback of *Fifty Shades of Grey* and a can of masala powder. There was a small bottle of organic eucalyptus oil, a must to fend off the London cold. Two hand-woven scarves from Assam, one for her friend Sophie and one for her uncle's girlfriend. A wooden puzzle for Sophie's son Brendon. And finally, a miniature chess set from Amritsar for her uncle.

Catherine sat on the floor and sorted her laundry while Mr Darcy idled aside.

She had already given Mick his souvenir – a pair of handmade dance shoes.

Having finished her unpacking, Catherine stood up and looked at the mess below.

*Something was amiss.*

*Aha!*

Catherine had a flash of a memory. Where was the jaggery she had bought for Cecil? She bent over once again and ferreted around the nearly empty suitcase. Having no luck there, she stood up, stomping her feet.

*Must have left it in the office…*

Catherine winced then laughed at her carelessness. She would only hope that it made an excellent farewell present for her colleagues.

The house phone rang again. She went up and checked the caller.

*Speaking of the…*

Catherine shook her head. Her uncle must have informed Cecil of her return. She'd rather her uncle and her godfather paid less concern over her affairs.

Without waiting for the message, Catherine picked up the handset.

"What a wonderful delight." Cecil employed a calm tone. "I had thought you would refrain from answering my calls, Catherine. Like you did with Alex."

"Did he call? I'm not sure if I heard it." Catherine swallowed nervously.

"Well. Now that I have your attention…" Cecil's voice was steadfast. Sometimes she wondered if he would only show his powerful eloquence in court. "Let us sort the circumstances. One year ago, you told us that you needed some time to yourself and you embarked on a trip to India. Might I suggest that now the time has arrived for you to reconsider your options? I would dare to say that we would very much hope to see you settled, Sophie as well. Please do not let one man's *mens rea* trouble you anymore."

Catherine wanted to retort but quickly lost herself in swirls of thoughts.

A year.

Was it too long or too short? Too long to be away and too quick to forget?

*Out of sight, out of mind…*

In a mere year, her status had changed from being engaged, to one-day-nearly-wed, to single. She could not say that she had spent her year away in vain, but she could not positively claim that it had been fruitful either.

*Swoosh* came the sound of a fountain pen signing.

"Now that you are back from your volunteering post, I would suggest you could acquire some hands-on experience in the corporate world. There is an administrative position at the Chamber. Take a few days to catch your breath, and I'll see you in my office next Monday." Cecil now sounded like he was commanding a subordinate.

"I do appreciate the offer, but Cecil, I'm not a programmed robot, and I'll not act like one."

Catherine felt a surge of anger rise within her. Then she felt something rubbing against her right foot. She looked down and found Mr Darcy nibbling on her trouser leg. She recalled her friend Mick's words from an hour ago: 'We left early, and Mr Darcy didn't get any breakfast. Remember to feed him when you get back home'.

"I'm sorry. Listen, Cecil, I've just got back now, and I'm exhausted. Perhaps we could discuss it later? Not the post, I mean. Dinner plans." She slowed her speech. "Maybe I'll find something better within the week, like writing film commentaries. I've heard there's a digital publication in Soho looking for editors, and their offer is quite decent."

Catherine followed Mr Darcy to the kitchen. She found an unopened bag of cat food and poured some into Mr Darcy's food plate.

"That's a topic we can moot. If by 'decent', you mean that they are offering you the London living wage, then I doubt it was indeed a decent offer and not a paltry one." Cecil was quick to see through her excuse. "Alex and I have made a promise to take care of you and take care of you we will. Your parents would want you to live a life free of worries."

Her mouth suddenly tasted bitter upon hearing these words.

Her uncle and Cecil would always bring up her parents, who had passed away years ago in a car accident, to inculcate their plans with her.

Catherine tried to steer away from this conversation. "Why do I feel that

Mr Darcy has put on weight again? I'd say we need a three-month diet regime," she muttered to herself as much as to Cecil. Her eyes drifted across the kitchen and fixed upon a cute cat calendar hanging on the refrigerator door. The calendar still showed the month of April 2014. The 25th had a heart drawn around it in a pink highlighter with a small Post-it next to it: 'Birthday & Wedding'.

*As if I were a blind dog hunting a deer...*

Catherine had recalled a Punjabi proverb. A villager told her it meant that an incompetent person could not bring herself to do a tough job.

*Such an accurate description.*

On the evening before her wedding, when Catherine had found out that Pierre had been cheating on her, she ran off to India without any confrontations. She wondered if it was because she couldn't bear to hear her fiancé confess to a loss of interest after having promised her a life-long love. Or perhaps she nurtured faint illusions that Pierre would eventually follow her and come halfway around the world to find her. To get on his knees and tell her that he was truly sorry.

Catherine had waited and waited some more. No call of apology, no message of repentance, only a returned engagement ring, delivered to her uncle but lost in transit.

*Not the best birthday present that I had ever received.*

At least now, she dared to make fun of the situation.

But did her past still beat inside her like a second heart?

Looking back, she realised their marriage would have been short-lived. She couldn't lie to herself.

"Cathy? Are you still there?" Cecil said, and Catherine pulled back her thoughts.

Mr Darcy had already finished his light meal and was licking his paws on the windowsill over the kitchen counter.

"Yes, I'm listening." Catherine bit her lip and replied, "Let me think about the work. I'm tired, and I want to get some sleep."

"Good. Get plenty of rest. I'll pick you up tonight, and we can go to dinner. Alex wants to introduce his new *inamorata* to you."

Just as Cecil was speaking, a succession of loud bangs startled Catherine.

A large man in a black bucket hat and green raincoat stood outside her kitchen window. He raised his head; a deep centipede-shaped scar crawled on the left side of his face.

The man drummed on the window with his fists while shouting incomprehensively.

With a final, heavy blow, a long crack formed, and the window glass shattered.

Mr Darcy's tail puffed up, and Catherine screamed.

* * *

How long had it been since she'd ended the call?

A minute?

Ten seconds?

An hour?

Holding Joyce's cold body, as cliched as it might sound, Tilly had lost all sense of time.

She tried to move her arm, only to find that she was not even wearing her watch.

*What if…*

What if she had never replied to Joyce's text?

A rambling of footsteps echoed in the room. The cleaner had returned.

"They're here."

Sound travelled through a sea of emotions and finally broke into Tilly's muffled ears. She looked up mechanically and saw a man and a woman appearing in the bedroom's doorway.

She could hear ambulance sirens faintly in the distance.

"Would you please step away?" a middle-aged man asked softly.

Perhaps it was not the first time he had to witness such an occasion.

Tilly stood up; her legs felt like overcooked spaghetti.

There was a piece of A4 paper on the dresser. On it was printed a line: *This is not goodbye.*

But she knew Joyce would never wake again.

# CHAPTER 3

"Thank you." Changxi Yang tucked away his passport and moved through the automated glass gates at Border Control in Heathrow Terminal 5.

He followed the signs for baggage reclaim and took the elevator downstairs.

A ruckus appeared before his eyes as travellers searched for their luggage.

He looked at the LED screen overhead – six forty-five p.m.

*Just on time.*

A family stood near the information counter and inquired about their missing bags.

He checked the monitor, walked to area number nine, and moved his stiff shoulders. The airport ceiling had decorations of silver metal discs, overlooking the commotion below.

The conveyor belt crept slowly.

Nearby passengers swarmed around like meerkats, each occupying a vantage point. Someone rolled a luggage cart on top of his right heel.

He stepped forward, and the pressure was gone.

It did not take long for his black carry-on to come out.

He carried his suitcase to the exit. No one paid attention to him, and no one bothered to check his luggage ticket.

*'Gotta raise a little hell!'* A song by Dorothy played.

He put in his earphones and continued his path. He pocketed his boarding pass and headed for the green lane under 'nothing to declare' for Customs.

Another automatic metal door, and he found himself surrounded by duty-free shop assistants trying to sell pungent perfumes. He shook his head lightly and walked out.

Scattered rows of people stood in front of the Arrivals exit. Cab drivers held pieces of paper with names awaiting their passengers. Others waited for family and friends.

A group of travellers parted like a herd of animals. Some hugged with reverence; some travelled across to the Heathrow Express ticket machine, some went to Marks & Spencer's.

He put down his suitcase and looked around, searching the crowd. He spotted his target: Felipe Kazama was sitting comfortably not far away, legs crossed, engrossed in a *National Club Golfer* magazine.

"*Otsukare\**." Felipe finished skimming the magazine and waved at him.

The eldest son of an indigenous mother and a Nikkei father in Peru, Felipe Kazama had cauliflower ears and deep eyes. He wore a sheepskin jacket, and his hair looked as if a dog had licked it.

Chance moved his lips but didn't say anything.

Only this morning, Felipe had summoned him to take the earliest flight from Tokyo to London. And Chance Yang was someone who disliked haste.

"Did you use the famous line?" Felipe laughed. "The Oscar Wilde quote: I have nothing to declare but my genius?"

Chance shook his head and responded sternly, "I took the non-declaration route."

"Good to have a joke after a long flight, no? Give me a sec to call the driver."

Felipe took out his phone, made a call, then dropped the magazine in a bin.

Chance took off his earphones, arranged them neatly, and stashed them in his shirt pocket.

"Still using the old trick, I see." Felipe said. "I have to say that pretending to be listening to music is not the best way to dodge conversations."

"Someone was listening to rock full blast. It didn't do any harm to shield my ears against it." Chance took out his boarding pass from his shirt pocket and refolded it.

Felipe had a look. "Economy? Not quite your style."

Chance smiled bitterly. "Not bad, considering it was the last seat available."

Felipe glanced at his luggage. "You know, the only purpose luggage tags serve is to say to malicious individuals: hey, here's my suitcase, and these are my details. Why don't you come and blackmail me? Did you know that blackmail and harassment are the top two reported crimes in the Square Mile?"

A ringtone told Felipe that their car was coming.

Chance followed him upstairs to Departures. A silver Range Rover rested close to the kerb. Felipe opened the left door and slid into the passenger seat. Chance stowed his suitcase, saw the 'no passenger pickup' sign across the road, got in, sat down, and buckled his seatbelt.

"Let me introduce you." Felipe turned his head. "This is Johnson from the London division. This is Chance Yang. We worked together on a merger in Osaka."

A rather handsome young man in the driver's seat greeted Chance and started the car.

A few minutes passed. Felipe busied himself on his phone. Johnson had turned on the radio. 'Muskrat Love' by the Captain & Tennille played, followed by a news item on the Holborn fire's aftermath.

Chance lowered the window on his side. Warm, humid air pressed to his face. In the distance, anvils of storm clouds gathered, and the sun's scintillations leaked like a flashlight from a keyhole. He had escaped London six years ago, and now he was back.

"Did you bring me the item I requested?" Felipe asked him in Japanese when their car passed the large Porsche shop.

*No messages. It seems Johnson does not understand the language…*

Chance looked at Johnson's frazzled face; he looked no more than twenty-five years old.

"Yes, I have it with me."

The item in question was the latest issue of *Shonen Jump*, a Japanese comic magazine.

"Good." Felipe nodded. "Here are three adjectives to describe horrible weather: stormy, rainy, and British." He tapped quickly on his phone. "Oh, I've got an email. Let me reply first. Thank you for the update…Huh. You always have to say this, even if the crap they have sent caused hell for you. And 'yours faithfully', ugh, how can you be faithful to someone whom you've never met?" He continued. "When I first read *Hellsing*, I didn't expect to end up in London one day. It was rumoured that when Hirano Kouta came to London to look for inspiration, the local folks maltreated him. The hotel's concierge discriminated against him, and the food was…You know the torture better than I do. And just when he thought he had met a kind person, that someone sold him a bogus souvenir. I feel for him. I do. I was like, isn't it a replica of my Tokyo experiences? Tragedies are all alike."

Chance leaned back into his seat. The well-maintained leather seats felt good to touch. He yawned with a hand over his mouth. A drizzle smudged his view. Raindrops merged into a stream on the glass, then escaped quickly like tadpoles swimming away. He rubbed his face and observed Johnson from between his fingers. There was something odd about the way he gripped the steering wheel. Perhaps Johnson was a bike rider.

Chance could not resist his curiosity and asked the one question he had been contemplating since he boarded his flight. "Why did you ask me to come over in such a hurry?"

"This is not the right venue to answer your question." Felipe smiled back and answered in English. "Not in the car, anyway." He took out a dark brown eye mask from the glove box and arranged it on his head. "A neighbour upstairs has a mad dog that barks every night and day. There's another guy who likes to watch live football. He screams like he's having an orgasm whenever his team scores a goal. These disturbances have led to severe sleep insufficiencies for me. Let me catch a little shut-eye. I can brief you tonight." Felipe adjusted his seat and lowered himself comfortably.

Johnson turned off the radio on cue. The only sound was rain dancing on glass and occasional car horns.

Chance loosened his seatbelt and leaned his face against the window. Lost in the scenery passing by, he thought he had seen a familiar face of someone who died six years ago.

\* \* \*

*Half an hour later.*

"Morning, sunshine. We're here."

The car came to a halt.

Chance opened his dazzled eyes and saw his door was open. Felipe stood in front of him. "I thought if you didn't wake up, I could help you with an ice bucket challenge."

Many people had warned Chance that Felipe liked to engage in horseplay. Felipe held a bottle of mineral water in his hand, and he did not look as though he was joking. Chance removed his seatbelt and patted his face before slipping out of the car.

The rain had stopped, and the air smelled like greasy KFC's fries. Not that he wouldn't fancy some.

He took his luggage from Johnson, looked around, and found himself standing in a small courtyard surrounded by a black metal fence. A two-way, double-lane road lay beyond the waist-high wooden gate at the entrance. There were several shops across the street: a dry cleaner's, a Turkish kebab house, a restaurant, and a small hardware store, all with a common word on their fronts: 'Oval'.

"I'll head back to the office. Call me if you need anything." Johnson smiled as if he was rushing to a date. He reinstated himself in the driver's seat and waved his hand. "See you tomorrow morning."

Felipe waved back while Chance remained confused.

After the Rover turned and disappeared, Felipe pointed to the inconspicuous, three-storey grey brick building behind them. "Follow me."

Chance nodded.

Their company had rented the second-floor flat on the east-facing side for them.

Passing through the dark and poky hallway, Chance almost tripped over a children's tricycle. He carried his suitcase and carefully followed behind Felipe, stepping on narrow stairs as if designed for tightrope walkers and acrobats.

*One…two…*

After fifteen similar tortures, Felipe unlocked the apartment door and motioned Chance to go in first.

Once inside, he found himself facing a small bathroom. The flat would not have been a Chinese tenant's favourite pick: bathrooms facing doors were a Feng shui taboo.

A small door next to the bathroom was half-hidden, allowing a peek through to the five-square-metre kitchen.

It was just a usable flat with no frills.

One single bed in the left-hand bedroom was stacked with shopping bags from designer brands. A fake fireplace adorned the living room. A settee sat in the middle, looking as though it had been scavenged from a local tip, with a family pack of barbecue-flavoured hula hoops on top. A few books were scattered around: *Histories* by Herodotus, *The Passions of the Soul*, and a mystery by Natsuhiko Kyogoku.

"Arf-arf! Arf-arf!" A dog barked in the hallway. Most likely, the culprit that had upset Felipe.

"Mr Grey! Do slow down! The park will still be there!"

They heard a woman's voice, followed by the sound of steps going downstairs.

"Not bad, eh?" Felipe asked sardonically. "Especially for people who dislike living in hotels. I told you Mercury has great perks." He smiled slyly. "The bad news is…there's only one key, and I'm keeping it so you can't go clubbing all night. Curfew at ten." Felipe leaned against the door. "Just joking. I've made you a spare."

Chance set his suitcase next to the settee. He was glad that he had packed his sleeping bag. He was also pleased that the settee cover wasn't the white colour that he hated so much.

There was a paper shredder in the corner. Chance took out his boarding ticket and fed it into the machine.

"Now, it's quite late." Felipe looked at his Rolex Daytona. "Why don't we go out and get a bite first?"

"I'll wash my face." Chance took off his jacket and walked into the bathroom as he rolled up his shirt sleeves.

The floor creaked as he stepped away.

In the bathroom, he found a cockroach near a corner under the bathtub. He pretended not to see it, trying not to think whether it was dead or alive.

There was a bottle of Ipecac syrup on the washbasin.

He turned on the tap, and cold water rushed out with rust. He took a handful and buried his face in it.

The square mirror above the washbasin was missing a corner. He patted his face dry and looked at himself in the mirror.

It had only been one day, yet he felt so much exhausted.

*See what London does to you.*

He stepped out of the bathroom and found Felipe idling on the settee, chewing on a hula-hoop-shaped snack.

"Let's go." Chance put on his jacket. The sky outside their small window had already turned cobalt blue.

"Yes, let's go." Felipe put down his snack and swiped the bits away. "Ah! I almost forgot." He walked into the bedroom, found his beavertail sap, and tucked it behind his waist. "I hope we don't run into that mad dog," he exclaimed with resentment.

After a light dinner at the Turkish place across the street, they decided to stroll around the neighbourhood.

Stopping at Clapham Road, they turned left at the junction into Harleyford Road. The giant stadium, the Oval, on the side of the road hosted cricket matches. A few bright stadium lights within the red brick walls of the Oval shone their way. On this no-match night, the place was eerily silent, like the lair of a monster in a horror film.

"Have you ever played cricket?" Felipe asked while zipping his sheepskin jacket.

"Tried it once in university. I wasn't good at it."

"Baseball?"

"Tried it in high school, though I never made a strike."

Felipe nodded.

An empty beer can stood on the deserted pavement. Felipe kicked it into a bin five metres away. "Well. I'm more of a soccer person."

A ship's horn sounded in the distance. The two walked in silence for a while and made their way to Vauxhall Bridge. The evening rush had started.

Queuing cars crawled slowly across the bridge, and the bike lanes were like clogged water pipes. The mysterious MI6 headquarters was not unlike an Aztec temple, while the shadows of the riverfront buildings in Chelsea swayed in the water like origami made from Kanazawa gold leaf.

The smell of freshly picked mushrooms permeated the evening air.

"Albert Camus once noted, as a remedy to life in society, I would suggest the big city. It's only been a few days, but I think I've fallen in love with London already. A city steeped in history," Felipe confessed. "Some say that New York is an oil painting, a 'Big Apple'. Others say that New York is a verb, people coming and going trying to make a living. And London is a noun, with the Houses of Parliament, Buckingham Palace, the London Eye, the Shard, the parks, Wimbledon, the Queen, and Sherlock Holmes. The list of attractions never ends. Even a view from this bridge is a watercolour."

"A Chinese poet once wrote, when you regard the view from a bridge, others regard you as their view\*," Chance mused.

"Perhaps a better way to put it is when you envy others, not knowingly, they envy you as well." Felipe leaned on the railing, "Johnson told me that I could see St Paul's Cathedral from here."

"From here?" Chance hesitated. "If you prefer a terminal vista, then perhaps the Millennium Bridge is better."

"The wobbly one?" Felipe laughed. "Let me enlighten you. You can see the full view from here as well." He looked around and pointed to a bridge pillar not far to his left. "See for yourself."

Chance gripped the railing with both hands and reached out to look. He saw a statue, like a goddess from Greek mythology. The statue held something like a small model of a house in its hand. On closer inspection, it was a miniature of St Paul's Cathedral.

"Legend has it that two engineers insisted on adding eight statues for aesthetic reasons during the reconstruction of the bridge. Each of them managed one sector, like science and agriculture. This one happens to be on a straight line with the Cathedral on a map; hence it's responsible for architecture," Felipe expounded. "That's what Johnson told me, anyway. Quite a sharp chap."

Chance nodded. "I can see that."

"Speaking of churches, we have to mention slightly annoying associations: funerals." Felipe smiled. "The reason why you are here has to do with a funeral as well. Two weeks ago, a client's sister died in her apartment. I heard it was suicide."

"And you suspect that it was not?" Chance asked gingerly.

"No, no." Felipe smiled again, showing his teeth. "You probably won't believe it. I know this client. He's a staunch atheist. But he told me that on the night of the seventh day of his sister's passing away, he had the strangest dream he had ever had. He saw his sister kneeling at his bedside, saying that she wanted him to help her."

"And?"

"And that's why you are here." Felipe shot him a meaningful glance. "Mercury mainly deals with financial services, but these types of... unfortunate undertaking appear from time to time like pimples on an angel's arse, as John Barth would say. Many times, I've had to wipe the asses of deceased clients, like taking care of pets or making dodgy donations. I even ghost-wrote a PhD thesis for a debauchee. 'Global Governance' is such a parroted topic. I would rather people put in some hours and try to find a cure for Thalassemia. Remember our philosophy? When clients ask, we deliver."

"I'm not sure what you want me to do." Chance sighed.

"Let me walk you through the situation first." Felipe thought for a while. "The client is from China. The deceased was his half-sister, Joyce Peng, who had studied in England and later returned to Shanghai. She was diagnosed with a brain illness and had an operation earlier this year. She got back to London at the end of March and was found dead on the 6th of April."

"And the cause of her death?"

They walked and talked.

"It appeared that she'd learnt from online sources to overdose on codeine, but the immediate cause was more likely her choking on her own vomit." Felipe coughed softly. "I've seen photos of the scene. She even tied a plastic bag over her head...quite a distressing picture that reminded me of Heaven's Gate."

"I don't see where I come into contributing."

"Quite simple," Felipe said as they made way into a pedestrian tunnel, and he stared at a wall with paintings of blue skies and fleecy clouds. "I want you to trace her whereabouts before her death, check her card transactions, go to her apartment, talk to people she'd met, find out if she tipped generously, if she cried with abandon, if she hugged strangers, if she bought any *Big Issues*? There are so many ifs. The devil is in the detail. The expenses for this side hustle will all be reimbursed. The client's father, upon hearing of his daughter's passing, suffered a severe heart infarction. Surely you wouldn't deny a dying man's last wish?"

Sometimes, Chance found Felipe had more front than the Houses of Parliament.

"You'll have two months." Felipe diverted his eyes from the clouds to Chance. "You know, I'd say it's quite a catch. If I knew Chinese, I would have offered myself for the role."

Chance remained silent. He feared for more.

"Now, let's put the deceased aside and discuss the still-living ones." Felipe took out his phone, tapped on the screen, and handed it to Chance. "Have a look."

He took the phone. On the screen was a picture of someone's kitchen. The glass window was broken, and the sink was bloody.

"An acquaintance to whom I owe a favour, his goddaughter was recently harassed by a stalker. The man tried to break into her house. He asked me to find someone capable to oversee her safety." Felipe's eyes glazed over like a child who had been pranking on the neighbour's doorbell and hadn't been caught. "I told him I knew the perfect person for the job."

Chance took a breath and held up his hands in desperation. "I can deal with cross-referencing card transactions. I can deal with browser histories. I do *not* wish to become someone's bodyguard."

"Can't say for certain that it isn't unrelated to the job in hand." Felipe suddenly became serious. "The girl's uncle was Joyce Peng's personal tutor at college. Say you do him a favour; he might be able to assist."

They walked back to their apartment and bumped into the neighbour from upstairs. She was a slight chubby lady of about sixty, with neither promising features nor flaws. Her dog, Mr Grey, was a Chihuahua. Chance was puzzled. How could such a small dog have such a loud bark?

"Lady first," Felipe said cheaply after opening the hallway door.

The neighbour eyed them suspiciously and murmured a vague thank you.

There were a few letters in their mailbox. Felipe picked them up and read them, pocketing one of them.

"An estate agent came to see me the other day and asked if I'd like to sell the house. I told him that he needed to get his sources together. I'm just a tenant. How can I have the right to sell him the house?"

Felipe opened the door, and Chance followed him. "Then a few days later, another one knocked on my door, I thought another huckster maybe, so I decided to ignore him, but he was rather insistent, like an NHK fee collector. I asked him what he wanted. He said he needed me to provide some information so as not to delay voting. Then I told him that we were only a couple on our honeymoon and had acquired our short-term accommodation from Airbnb. No one bothered me after that." Felipe smiled. "And I got some first-hand knowledge of the constant discrimination that the LGBTQ+ community in London experiences daily. The neighbours look at me as if I escaped from the zoo."

Chance unpacked as Felipe recounted his stories.

Later, Felipe picked up his books from the couch and went into the bedroom.

Chance thought for a while and knocked on the bedroom door. "We need to talk."

Felipe was ironing his shirt. "You may talk all you want. I reserve the right not to respond. Or to listen at all."

"I don't mind digging around in someone's past. But I'm not capable nor willing of being anyone's bodyguard," Chance mumbled. "Remember Mexico City? I made mistakes that nearly got someone kidnapped. How do you expect me to protect someone else?"

"Not so much a grand gesture like that. Call it…assisting."

"I think…"

"You may think all you like, and I'll not change my mind." Felipe put down the iron. "Where there's a will, there's a way. I've signed you up for a four-day Krav Maga Bootcamp. Jujitsu does not suit you, but Krav Maga might be the right choice for self-defence for you."

Felipe pointed to a nylon bag from SportsDirect. "Picked up some sportswear this morning. Also, I got you a new iPhone, the latest model. Better not waste our client's goodwill. It's good to be a butter-and-egg man once in a while."

Chance sighed and took the bag. The phone was still in pristine packaging.

"I chose you. Because you are tight-lipped, and you've spent time in London." Felipe looked at him. "There's always a home advantage in sports. Johnson will pick you up tomorrow morning. Ouch!"

He cursed and licked his finger. "Has it ever happened to you? One day, you discover a small cut on your right hand. You had no idea how it happened. Then two or three days later, you find another cut on your left hand. You promise to watch out. Then you have another cut..." Felipe continued to complain as he ironed the rest of his laundry.

Eventually, the task was done, and the conversation ended.

Snuggling in his sleeping bag and listening to the sound of traffic and rain outside, sleep came slowly to Chance. The springs of the old settee beneath him poked in all ways possible.

Felipe had called New York a verb and London a noun. Chance tried to recall his life in London six years ago, but everything came down to one rainy scene. For him, London was only a disconcerting adjective.

He closed his eyes. He could only remember the summer of his final year of university when his stepmother Lynette came to visit: their conversation at the new Heathrow terminal and his plans after graduation.

Then fate had struck him as if he'd been shot from behind.

That summer. His father's lung cancer recurred not long before Isabel died of a drug overdose. Everyone who knew her recognised it as a most heart-breaking incident.

That summer was his childhood's end.

\* \* \*

The next day, before breakfast, Felipe took out a file folder and tossed it onto the table. "This is for you. Some material Johnson compiled. Might be useful."

Chance put on his Omega Constellation, opened the folder, and spilt its contents onto the table. There was a copy of Joyce Peng's credit card history, a notebook, an iPhone, and a sheet of A4 paper. On the paper was printed a line: This is not goodbye.

"I really can't understand the so-called Generation Z. Or what's the latest term? Generation Snowflake? Even their suicide notes are preposterous. I'd have left explicit instructions on how to destroy all my electronic devices and digital trail," Felipe buttered his toast. "I once read a book; one sentence touched me deeply. The author said that he does not wish depression on his worst enemy." He took a bite, and his masseter muscle jerked. He looked out of the window. "Johnson's still not here. I called, and he didn't answer. I left him a voicemail."

"What's the passcode for her phone?"

"0909. Her birthdate; quite simple."

Chance unlocked the phone. "People don't care enough about personal data security."

"Did you hear about the breach when someone charged their vape on their work laptop? There was malware on the USB." Felipe laughed. "Many people carry a bug with them. They don't realise it. Not yet. I even found Al Gore's telephone number on S&P Capital IQ once."

A quick inspection of the calling history informed Chance that there had been a dozen missed calls on the morning of 6th April from the same caller. There were a few missed calls, messages, and voicemails from the brother, Jayden, on the afternoon of the 5th. He browsed through the message history. Nothing particularly drew attention.

"I've heard that she was never on good terms with her father's side of the family. Jayden has been making peace on both ends." Felipe arranged the creases in his shirt. "You know there was a major fire in Central London, right?"

"The in-flight newspaper covered it quite extensively." Chance picked up the notebook. Something fell out: a ticket to a play on 1st April. *A View from the Bridge.* He wondered what bridge it was – a bridge in London, perhaps.

"It appeared that because of the fire, she was unable to stay in her apartment and she went to an old friend's house for a few days."

"Right." Chance skimmed the notebook contents. There were some calendar entries.

*30 March – Singing Taster Actors' Centre 14:00*

*1 April – A View from the Bridge 14:30*

*6 April – Cleaning 9:00*

"I surmise that she must have been shocked." Felipe leaned back on the settee. "I forgot to mention that she went to seek refuge at an ex's place… and now the person is married."

Chance listened as he flipped through the diary pages. There were paragraphs written in English.

*Some people are often late, so they set their watches ten minutes faster to remind themselves not to be late. The digital clock on the oven was thirteen minutes faster, but I felt like I'd earned this time. It's like flying back to London. You always feel that you have gained a few extra hours of disposable time.*

*Even the LSE could not escape a manufactured risk.*

*Yesterday I met a couple in a restaurant. One of them told me that they didn't live together because he was afraid that the mundane bits of daily life could wear their love thin. He might be right.*

Another paragraph was written in a different colour.

*Perhaps I want to write something that everyone could write, so it is something that everyone could identify with it. But I also want to write something that not everyone could write, for it would take away my uniqueness. A story that doesn't tell that people who wear their watches on their left hands are left-handed, and a story not so simple as if you wear nail polish on your fingers, you won't leave fingerprints. Like a teacher who prepares a set of exam questions and who hopes the students can pass, but the questions can't be too easy either.*

\* \* \*

"I have a conspiracy theory concerning you," Isabel whispered. "Why do you wear your watch on your right hand? You're not left-handed."

He showed her the watch his stepmother had bought him. "The crown gave me a lump on the back of my hand, so I wear it the other way now."

"Ah. That's why." Isabel faked disappointment. "I had thought that aliens had secretly taken over and replaced you with a Bioroid."

"If I were one—" Chance made a face— "I wouldn't admit it, would I? Or what would happen to my mission?"

"I don't give a shit about your damn missions." She smiled bitterly. "Now, I want you to give me a shoulder massage. My job-hunting and exams have been driving me mad. A friend offered some Ritalin the other day. At this rate, I might even take some."

He sat upright and began to rub her shoulders.

"If I were an alien, I'd have used my superpower to increase my bank balance by a dozen or so zeroes, like what happened in *Sin Noticias de Gurb*. We could buy an island, have many cats, and spend the rest of our lives there."

"That's easy for you to say," she sighed. "But let's do something good for humanity as well. Why don't we go to South America and let everyone have free universal healthcare, then hire many lobbyists to legalise abortion."

"Relax," he massaged her neck in circles.

"I like your massages…you are indeed my *remedio chino*, like in Manu Chao's song…and it doesn't cost a penny."

"But if no one spends money, the economy will die." He borrowed a line from his stepmother.

\* \* \*

"Hey! Señor! Still with me, or did something get you? Johnson did tell me that this house was once a burial ground."

Chance pulled his thoughts together. Felipe stared at him.

"No. I'm quite alright." Chance hesitated. "Probably the jet lag." He closed the diary. "You were saying she did it on impulse? I'm not sure, but I do know that codeine is a prescription drug. It would take some time to prepare, for one thing."

"That's the issue at hand." Felipe opened a portable aluminium ashtray and lit a cigarette. "She stole it from her ex. The whole thing is too complicated, with too many coincidences. No one expected a fire. No one expected her to stay over at her ex's, and no one expected that the ex had some toxic assets in stock."

"Just because the ex is married…isn't that a bit far-fetched? They'd been split for some years, right?"

"Have you not heard that the heart is a random place and a lonely hunter?" Felipe cautioned sternly. "One good thing about finance is that if there's no investment, there's no return. *Nada.* It's a different story with love. It seems that you still don't have much grasp about the mental state of people who commit suicide."

"You know it well then, I suppose?"

"Well enough," Felipe admitted. "I attempted it once. In middle school, when I was too young to know any better, I swallowed forty aspirins over a…an incident. Unfortunately, or should I say, fortunately, my old man found me and force-fed me water from a cattle hose. Not the best gastrolavage experience I've had. He's so relieved to save a pair of hands. My *ikigai* was probably worth a Mahindra. Anyways, I escaped death by a hair's breadth. Hmm, it rhymes." He smiled faintly. "Did you know that there's a golden fifteen minutes to intervene before someone commits suicide? Fifteen minutes, you can make a difference. Yet, those who are eager to die would act in five. You think about it, and you execute. I wish the Japanese banking system were so efficient. Marquez once compared love to a deadly liver disease that could trigger a complication called suicide. And they say that writers are a profession with a high suicide rate. Have you ever heard of this story? A girl who crosses a toll bridge paid half the price; then the guard asks her why and she announced she only intended to go halfway. We should be glad that Joyce Peng used medication rather than jumping off anything. Stats have shown that women tend to use poison more often than men to kill themselves – or others. Do you know why, when people jump off buildings, they tend to remove their shoes?"

Chance remained silent.

"Could it be they feel that they have exhausted every other option and have no other way to go, or maybe they leave them there, so people notice? Once – it was the plum rainy season in Japan, I believe – I took off my canvas shoes and put them out on the balcony to dry. My landlady saw, and she slapped me right in the face, shouting that 'life is a sacred thing! *Bakayarou!*' I was dumbfounded. I plead guilty to that once when I was a kid in Peru, but I've never thought about it again. What doesn't kill you might not make you any stronger, but it changes you for sure. Do you know which country has the highest suicide rate in the EU? First place goes to Lithuania. Hmm…I believe this knowledge might come in handy for you one day. You can thank me when the occasion arrives." Felipe stood up and checked his phone. "Okay. We'll discuss this later. Johnson should be here soon. Off you go now."

Chance put the items back into the folder when an alarm sounded on Joyce Peng's phone.

He disabled the alarm and turned the phone off, remembering doing the same with Isabel's phone six years ago. Neither of their owners needed to keep track of time anymore. He had felt a strange connection with the now deceased.

*Perhaps all things happen for a reason…*

The Rover appeared in his peripheral vision.

He made to leave.

✳ ✳ ✳

*Half an hour later.*

"57 Rossmore Road. Should be around here…" Johnson eased on the brake and examined the buildings from left and right. "I updated the sat nav yesterday."

A car behind them flashed its headlights impatiently.

"You can leave me here." Chance looked at his watch.

"I'm really sorry." Johnson pulled over to the side. "I have to fetch Mr Kazama for golf."

"No worries. I'll see you this afternoon."

Chance left the car and removed his sports bag from the trunk. A set of golf clubs sat there along with a motorbike helmet from Brough Superior.

He walked around and found a church at 57 Rossmore Road, which didn't look like the place he was after. He carried his gym bag, waited for a red light, and crossed the street to a residential complex called Palgrave Gardens.

A security guard stood at the gate.

"Sir, excuse me." He took off his sunglasses. "Do you know a place where you can learn self-defence around here?"

The man didn't reply, just pointed haphazardly to the right with a thumb.

"Thanks."

Chance found a massage parlour that was out of business. A sign stood next to the shop.

*75 Rossmore Road, self-defence Bootcamps, this way →*

He tucked his sunglasses away and walked in. There was an old garage now converted into training ground behind.

"Hello. Here for Bootcamp?" A well-built, feisty fellow stood outside the door and greeted him. He wore a grey sweatshirt with shorts and camouflage-themed training shoes. His pecs looked bigger than his face.

Chance held out his hand. "Morning."

"Dominic Turner." The man shook his hand vigorously. "Call me Turner."

"Nice to meet you. I'm Chance."

The thirty-square-metre training ground hosted a stench of sweat as if fifty athletes who had completed a marathon had stayed there overnight.

"Don't worry about it. Some air fresheners would do." Turner seemed to have noticed his concern. "It seems that the ventilation system is down."

Chance nodded, but he knew that this was a smell that had already tainted every wall in the room. Even the most wonderful air freshener would not work its magic. He picked up his gym bag and pointed to the changing room on the side. "I'll go and change."

"Okay." Turner smiled.

After a few minutes, Chance stepped onto the sponge mats and took a deep breath. "I guess we can start? I know nothing about Krav Maga."

Turner stared at him in confusion. "I thought you were the coach. Are you not?"

Chance was surprised. "I thought you were the coach."

They eyed each other and finally laughed.

"Sorry, mate. Made a mistake, I'm here for the Bootcamp too." Turner flashed a laugh; there was a small space between his front teeth.

Chance took note of the time. It was already five past nine. "Perhaps we can wait for a while."

"What made you want to do a Krav Maga course?" Turner asked as he sat on a pile of tyres and battle ropes.

"Well, work reasons, mostly. And you?"

Turner stroked his head. "I served in the Navy, and after that, I worked on a cruise ship for a few years around the world. When I got back, some friends said they're going to open a pub in Elephant and Castle and asked me if I wanted to be a part of it. We're worried that people might get carried away when drunk. I did take combat lessons before, and I hope to brush up on my skills. How about you? Correct me if I am wrong, but I reckon you're Chinese, in't you?"

"Yes, I am." Chance had expected some hostility, but Turner showed him none.

"I had many Asian passengers on that cruise, so I can tell where they're from, actually," Turner smiled. "And China! What a place! We went to many ports, Qingdao, Shanghai, Dalian. I went backpacking in China and India for a few months right after I got out of the Navy. The food there! I didn't want to leave. Though Chinese is so hard to learn. I once asked for soup in a restaurant, and they kept giving me sugar. Then another time, in Dalian, I tried to ask for directions but got slapped. I found out later that I confused the pronunciations of 'ask' and 'kiss'."

Chance chuckled. "I'm sorry to hear that."

As they conversed, a woman with two long braids arrived at the training area.

"You guys here for Krav Maga?" she asked as she hurried in.

"Yes. I'm Turner, and this is Chance." Turner took the initiative to make the introductions. "Are you also here for training? We're waiting for the instructor."

The woman laughed as she removed her bracelets and tied her hair up. "No more waiting, I promise." She stood upright. "I'm your trainer today. I'm Sidney. Sorry for running late. I was making some arrangements. Now that you're ready, follow me."

Sidney led them out of the alley to the front of the massage parlour.

"No more bush talking." She took out a timer. "Today, our first task is an attack drill. There is a gap on the right-hand side a hundred metres across the road. When you go in, you'll find a rectangular residential area where my colleagues are standing by. They are waiting to *ambush* you. Your mission is to cross the road, enter the area, and walk around the perimeter. It usually takes about five minutes to make the trip, so don't dawdle. Be on your guard. I've asked them to be kind."

The instructions had left Chance expressionless.

"Sounds pretty exciting." Turner rubbed his fists.

The instructor pointed across the road. "So, which one of you will have a go first?"

"I can do it," Turner volunteered. "There's only two of us. The sooner, the better, I'd say."

Chance watched as Turner crossed the road and disappeared into the residential area.

"The target's in. He's quite tall, wearing a grey sweatshirt, black shorts and a pair of Slazenger." Sidney gave Turner's description into a walkie-talkie.

Chance looked up at the passing clouds and tried to suppress his anxious thoughts.

Five minutes passed, but Turner was nowhere to be seen.

"Time's up. Your turn," came the instructor's icy voice. "Remember, don't dawdle."

Chance nodded and waited for the green light.

He crossed the road, found the small gap, descended a few stone steps, and entered the residential area.

It was a weekday; he had seen no one around the neighbourhood, but a few motorcycles and bicycles stood on the other side of the road.

He wondered who was waiting for him. He decided that it could be someone who looked weak.

He headed along the long side of the rectangle. Then, he continued his path and observed movements in front of him and behind him. He felt all his senses heightened.

A neighbouring house had closed windows, but he could still hear a stereo playing. In the distance, church bells were ringing. Two construction workers pulled lumber to a roof, buildings away. A helicopter circled overhead. He had never known that he could hear so well. His pulse echoed in his ears.

After an uneventful walk, he turned left into the short side of the rectangle.

A woman pushed a baby cart towards him. Could it be her?

He trod slowly, but the hairs on his neck stood up unwillingly.

The woman came up and stared at him intently.

He took a careful look at the baby cart. A baby that didn't resemble a doll slept under a blanket with Peter Rabbit patterns.

They walked on.

He wiped the beads of sweat with the back of his hand and continued to observe his surroundings.

A rather decrepit-looking old man with a stout walking stick stepped out of a shop onto the pavement, his hunched back somewhat unconvincing. Chance kept his distance from the man and felt relieved after he entered a building.

He had just put his mind at ease but noticed another figure reflected in a side mirror of a car parked nearby. The figure was moving fast and had something that resembled a long weapon in his hands.

*Here it comes!*

He stopped and ducked to the side of the road like a frightened pheasant, hiding behind a bus stop.

He waited and waited, but nothing happened.

No shouts, no actions, no suspicious figures in sight…

He poked his head out of his shelter and saw the man's back. He held a long umbrella, already hundreds of yards away.

*You're just paranoid.*

Chance took a breath and noticed the time; five minutes had passed already.

Nothing had happened. Yet.

He reached the end of the rectangle and found his way towards the training ground.

While he waited for the light, a black hatchback stopped beside him.

He clenched his fist as he observed with his peripheral vision.

The rear door opened, and a golden retriever dashed out.

# Chapter 4

"Anyway." Chance wiped his mouth with a napkin. "I asked Turner if anything happened to him. He said no as well. So, we went to the instructor. She explained that there was no ambush at all. She'd hoped that we could get a feeling of what would happen if we paid good attention to the surroundings." He sighed as he sipped a glass of mineral water. "So, we could feel the mental state of a person in stress."

"Isn't she quite something?" Felipe commented approvingly. He sliced a portion of octopus on his plate.

"The point being," Chance put down his glass, "We haven't learnt anything related to self-defence today. We spent the afternoon running in Regent's Park. She even asked us to write a short essay as homework to reflect on this morning's drill." He had a rather helpless expression on his face.

"No, that's not entirely accurate, I have to say." Felipe chewed the octopus carefully. "Didn't you learn a valuable lesson? That is, people are rather good at scaring the shit out of themselves. Before coming here, I watched a TV show in Japan. They claimed to have sightings of a *yokai** in the Fukuoka sky. They made it sound all mighty and scary. It turned out to be a piece of plastic mulch on the loose."

"Would you see it as appropriate if I waste my time writing essays and reflecting when someone is being stalked? Fine, I'll do the job. I can start tomorrow."

"That's not urgent for now." Felipe put down his knife. "Cathy went to Munich on business and won't be back until next week. Meanwhile, I'd suggest you take your time and commit yourself to your lessons." He smiled at Chance. "You were the one who didn't want the errand. And yet you are the one who's so eager now!" Felipe took up his knife again. "Let me offer you a piece of advice: never hold your thumb in your fist when you punch someone – you might break it."

Chance was about to demur when a waiter appeared with a glass of cranberry juice.

"Thank you. Can I have a straw, please?" He asked.

The waiter looked annoyed and cited his response by rote. "I'm sorry, sir. If plastic products receive no proper recycling, they will end up in the ocean and find their ways to the stomachs of turtles and fishes. To show our concern for the environment, we do not provide straws on our premises."

"That's fine. Thanks," Chance nodded.

They finished dinner in silence. Then Felipe requested the bill.

"I suppose you might want to add a tip, sir?" the waiter inquired.

"No, thank you." Felipe stood up and tossed his napkin across the table casually. "My dear friend, I take eating as a pleasure, not an opportunity for others to lecture me. Haven't you heard? If you're afraid of being raped, wear more clothes. If you're afraid of theft, bring nothing. If you're afraid of being murdered, die now. Knives and forks can kill, so why don't we stop using them? If you're afraid of plastic straws ending up in turtles' stomachs, then use paper ones, even steel ones. Don't shovel the problem to the customers."

The waiter retreated quietly to the kitchen as they left.

\* \* \*

*An hour later.*

Chance stared at a coffin resting in the middle of a diamond-shaped bar. Inside were racks of liquor bottles. Some bartenders sported bunny outfits but without the decorative tails. It was nine in the evening, and the bar was quite raucous. Laughter, noises, electronic music unknown to him, and the clinking of glasses mingled together in a maddening crowd.

"I told you about my day," Chance said. "Now tell me, how was golf?"

Felipe smiled. "It's a good experience, but the course's too small – only nine holes. I can't even use the joke that I'm going to the nineteenth hole." He watched as a shirtless bartender flirted with another. "Care for another drink?"

Chance rubbed his temples. "Yes, if they have any non-alcoholic options."

"How about a beer? The so-called adult soda?" Felipe laughed. "Just joking. I know you are quite committed to being teetotal. You still haven't told me why. However, I suspect that you wanted to condemn yourself for something, even as a self-punishment. Someone I know became a vegetarian simply because her parents died on a night when she refused to go to a vegetarian place with them. Well, Shakespeare named alcohol as an enemy that steals people's brains. Perhaps you are the wiser one." Felipe summoned a bartender. "Whiskey on the rocks and a cloudy apple juice."

"Right away." The bartender received Felipe's notes willingly.

"When you have time, perhaps we can go golfing together? It would make me feel top-hole to beat a former champion."

"Sure," Chance said wryly. "Even if I only won a children's tournament years ago."

"I can always adapt the story, can't I? John Nash never came up with the Nash equilibrium at a bar. It's a beautiful Hollywood adaption." Felipe stood up. "I'm going to the loo."

The drinks came. Chance opened the juice bottle and had a sip. It tasted more bitter than he remembered.

He had stopped drinking since Isabel's passing. A good friend once asked him why, and he could not quite explain it.

*Why drink if you cannot escape from a hangover that might last forever?*

He needed no more drinking.

\* \* \*

"What do you mean by a lobo?"

"No, not lobo! A law ball! We have a celebration tomorrow for the law faculty. You are coming?" Isabel brushed her hair quickly.

Chance replied while his fingers coded. "I think Kruz is throwing a party tomorrow night. I promised I would go. And you did say you were out of tickets...and I do need to finish this assignment."

"I got another from Mel. She had to go home, but I'm totally fine if you have other engagements."

He saved his files. "And I can't say that I enjoy talking with your colleagues."

"*Vale*," Isabel said sourly. "I might be able to find myself a better dance partner. I read a quote on The Student Room the other day: always order small portions of food, so you waste less; always pee after you've passed border control, or else the queue will be a long one; and always tell someone if you fancied them before graduation so that even if it didn't work out, you don't get to see each other that often and no awkward situation will present itself."

"You were saying?"

He ran his code. Still not working.

"I'm saying that a graduation is a milestone event, and someone might take advantage of another's vacillating state of mind."

Chance turned around on his swivel chair. "I can agree with the first and third points. But certainly not the second one. It might be bad for one's bladder if you try to hold on for too long."

\* \* \*

"That I agree with wholeheartedly." Felipe's voice slashed through his recollections. "It would be bad for your urinary system, indeed. But I do dislike toilets with UV lighting."

"Do they have it here?"

Felipe nodded.

"Wouldn't it be nice to prevent drug usage?" Chance paused. "I'm against all drug usage, and you're the one always saying we should come up with innovative problem-solving methods."

"Yes, problem-solving, not trouble-making. Once, they invited me to deliver a keynote speech at Todai*. I told them that my advice was never to go into finance – don't become the troublemakers but be the answer seekers. Finance is a liar-and-a-thief business." Felipe took a sip of his whiskey, the ice rocks no longer visible. "Theoretically, the blue light shines on the skin so drug addicts can't see the veins in their arms. It doesn't necessarily stop them. They could inject behind their knees. Does it solve the problem at hand at all? Rat Park tells us that drugs don't cause addiction but living conditions. As Cyril Connolly would say, everything's a dangerous drug to me except reality, which is unendurable."

Chance finished his juice. The jet lag, together with the training earlier that day, was making him drowsy.

"It's like handing out free, alcoholic mouthwash to the homeless and then having them drinking it instead of using it. When good intentions go awry, it's worse than bad plans executed well," Felipe commented. "Let me tell you something funny." His eyes twinkled. "Yesterday, I went out for a stroll after lunch. A woman stopped me halfway. She was in her early twenties, rather waif-like, and she asked me if I could lend her fifty quid. She gabbled, and I listened. She was desperate to go to a homeless shelter, had been sleeping rough for days. She assured me again and again that she wouldn't use the money on drugs, and she showed me her left arm, which didn't have any visible needle marks. Her skin was all sallow and pitted." He laughed. "I was going to ask her why she didn't show me her right arm but decided to hold my tongue. I gave her fifty quid and ran away like the wind. Perhaps I should have told her to save some money and migrate to Oregon, where marijuana is much cheaper than London. Did you know that Soho was an old hunting ground? She could also benefit from the right to collect roadkill to eat in the US." Felipe snorted. "See, I've been doing good deeds as well. Every time I meet the homeless, I remind them never to drink discarded Cola. Who knows what might be in there? To be good, you need to sacrifice yourself; to be superb, you need to sacrifice others. Think about Ryanair; they don't even give bottled water to their employees, whereas the too-big-to-fails gladly pay for their employees' pension plans. General Motors is only a pension management company with a hobby of making cars."

"I'm so beat now. Why don't you finish your drink so we can go back?" Chance yawned. "I still need to do my homework."

"The conscience of a good student as always? Never to leave any assignments unfinished?" Felipe joked. He moved closer and said discreetly in Japanese, "Hey, look at the guy on your right. There's something shifty about him."

Chance forced his sleepy eyes open and examined his neighbours. A man was chatting with a woman in a more than friendly way. He wore a blue suit with a pink-dotted pocket square. His companion had a red jacket and a white-lined black blouse, a black faux leather skirt, stockings, and black high heels. She also wore an elephant-shaped pendant.

"Did you see Zanya last Friday? She looked like she might peg out at any moment," the man said.

"That's hardly my business. Look, I'm going to powder my nose. Watch my bag for me."

"Of course, honey, I'll watch your bag…and your back as well."

As the woman in red left her seat, the man looked around. Checking that no one paid attention to him, he twisted open the decorative skull on his ring and spilt some powder into the woman's drink.

"I'll vouch that wasn't vitamins," Felipe commented. "Let's change seats."

"Sure." Chance had some idea of how events would unfold.

"Sorry to keep you waiting, hon." A few minutes later, the woman in red returned. She arranged her skirt and took her seat. "Just saw Tessie in the bathroom, that hussy! Always trying to drive a wedge between us!"

"We'll not let her bother us – not here, not again!" The man handed her the spiked drink. "This is our time. Cheers!"

"Cheers." The woman took the glass.

"Che-eers!" Felipe stood up suddenly and clinked his glass with the woman's, just in time to knock it away.

"Hey! What's wrong with you!?" The man was livid and stood up to dispute.

"Listen, buddy. I'm *soooo* sorry…" Felipe faked his drunken state to perfection. "No, no. I'm not drunk. I don't see the pink elephant yet. I'm only…a…little…tipsy…"

"Cut the crap!" The man almost roared over the small puddle by his feet. He grabbed Felipe's shirt collar.

"Honey, let him go." The woman tried to make peace. "I can get another one. Let's not have some trollied drunken arsehole ruin our night."

"Yes! Let's do that!" Felipe turned to the bartender and shouted, "another drink for the lady on me!" He took the woman's hand and planted a quick kiss, then leaned in close to examine her red nails. "Oooh! My darling, what beautiful nails you have! Could you possibly enlighten me as to which salon provided you with such an exquisite service?"

The woman drew her hand back nervously and tried to suppress a laugh. "Well…if you want to know, I did them myself following a tutorial on Instagram. I could show you the account if you're interested."

"Leave me alone with the sissy. I'll sort it all out." Her companion sounded more than a little impatient.

"Well…" Felipe turned towards Chance. "So, I've heard that in many US colleges, the schools provide the students with a nail polish that can tell if drinks are spiked or not. Is that true?"

"Quite true." Chance nodded. He disliked public attention, but he knew Felipe thrived on it. "If someone tries to put something in their drink when they go to the bathroom, they won't get away with it."

The woman had not missed the nuance of their conversation and slapped her date hard and fast.

"How dare you spoil my fun!" The man accosted and pressed Felipe firmly against the bar counter. "Listen, if you're not drunk enough, I'll let you have some more." He reached across the counter and grabbed a bottle of wine, ready to smash open Felipe's head.

"Ou...ch!"

The bottle did not shatter, but the man fell to the ground and groaned in pain.

Felipe re-tucked his leather sap behind his shirt. "Rumour has it that if you hit someone on the back of their knees, it hurts the most. So, I've seen it with my own eyes now." He grabbed the man's lapel and murmured in his left ear. "Now, buster, listen up. You're lucky that I'm in a good mood tonight. Think about it one more time, and I'll make sure you'll never find the need to wear a condom again."

"YOU WON'T FUCKING DARE!"

"If you have enough sense, then don't do yourself a mischief, try me, and you'll have no time to cry." Felipe pulled out his wallet, took out some fifty-pound notes, and shoved a few into the man's mouth. "Promise me you'll get some ointment."

Two bouncers arrived, and Felipe handed the notes to them. "Please, gentleman, do us the favour of removing this rubbish out of our sight."

They did so.

Mere minutes later, the club was restored to its previously lively state.

"Weren't you afraid they might throw you out?" Chance yawned and asked with bleary eyes.

Felipe smiled. "I forgot to mention that Johnson's a co-owner. Thanks to him, we have had a very entertaining evening. They say that in cities, antipathy protects you."

Chance shook his head and slapped his face lightly. "There's a saying in Chinese that passing dragons can't beat local snakes."

"Well, forensically speaking, he ain't a snake. More like an earthworm, I'd say." Felipe nurtured another drink. "I don't carry my leather sap for show and not for blow. Besides, combat is better practised one on one. He shouldn't really punch above his weight. Any pain is preferable to death. Have you ever heard the noise of bones cracking? I once read a book that declared it's the finest sound on Earth."

"Thank you for your help," the woman said.

"If helping others is a sacrifice, then I'm always willing to make that effort. Again, and again." Felipe grinned.

"I…I don't know what to say."

"Then don't say anything," Felipe replied without looking at her.

"But I wanted to say thank you…for just now," the woman spoke up. "My friend warned me before to be more careful, but I didn't believe her. I thought she was just jealous. I owe her an apology after all."

"Bastards exist every day, and today is no exception." Felipe waved his hand. "I heard that the nail polish that detects Rohypnol, Xanax, and GHB is available in the UK. You might as well look it up."

The woman imbibed her drink, the one Felipe had ordered. She noticed Chance and asked Felipe, "Is he your friend? Boyfriend? Let me buy you both a drink."

"Who?" Felipe turned around and patted Chance on his shoulder. "This stranger over here? I've only known him for an hour."

"No worries. I'm not drinking," Chance explained to the woman. "We work together. I'm the designated driver."

"You speak as if you brought a car." Felipe took another sip. "Listen, buddy. Next time when people offer to buy you a drink, and you wish to decline, don't say you don't drink, for that will only attract scorn; say you're in recovery – that'll get you sympathy." He turned to the woman in red. "I was filling out an online registration form earlier today. There was an option asking if I was homosexual or heterosexual. I'd hoped that there was a tick box for metrosexual, but there wasn't."

"You are quite…funny." The woman watched Felipe intently.

"I'm glad you didn't use the word 'interesting', for that would be an insult to me."

Chance listened as the two talked.

"Forgive me if I'm too forward. Are you seeing anyone?"

"Trust me, darling, I'd forgive you for anything," Felipe smiled. "The honest answer is yes. I have a girlfriend, but she's in another nation."

*Ah*, Chance thought as his eyelids drooped, and he fought sleep. *Not again.*

"Oh. Where is she?" A slight disappointment shone in the woman's eyes.

Felipe smiled again. "She's in my *imagination*. Care to fulfil it?"

"That's a funny way to say you're unattached."

"I dare not dent my pride or put the other party in an awkward position."

The woman flushed a little. "Perhaps we can start by getting to know each other a little bit more first?"

"Of course. The name's Felipe Kazama. Kazama is a Japanese word that means the time when wind passes – no, not passing wind, mind you. Hence my wuthering nature. Please call me Felipe."

"What do you do? Are you a martial arts instructor of a sort?"

"I'm a consultant."

"Sounds fancy."

"Nothing technical. To con and insult and to constantly affirm my bosses' biases. Once you learn the ins and outs, it's a bagatelle. Do you know who makes an ideal candidate for consultancy? Someone with average intelligence, someone who loves money, and someone who is willing to do *dirty* work."

"I'm Sara. Sara White." She reached out, and they shook hands gently.

Felipe didn't kiss her hand this time.

"Where are you from?"

Felipe smiled. "I'm from Earth. *Et toi?*"

"You *are* funny. I'm from Rochester."

"Rochester? It's a nice place."

"Have you been there?"

"No." Felipe winked. "But I've heard that all places ending with 'ster' are picturesque. Wouldn't you say so, kid?"

He turned to Chance and found that he had fallen asleep on the counter.

\* \* \*

"Morning, sleepyhead! Time to get up!"

A loud noise woke Chance, and he almost fell off the settee. It was already early morning. Sunshine seeped through the curtains.

"If you work for the World Bank, morning is the time when you start to think about how to screw up developing countries today. They don't admit it, but that's what they do *de facto*." Felipe tasted bitterness in his own words. "Many thanks to you for ruining my romantic night with Sara," he said as he drank his usual breakfast – three raw eggs. "You better hurry up. Johnson's already here."

Chance looked out of the window. A thin layer of fog blocked his view. The Rover's taillights glowed a dangerous hue. He remembered it was a foggy day when Isabel was found dead. Since he set foot in London, his memories of her had returned like a silkworm's threading effort.

He rubbed his eyes.

"Don't dawdle, as Sidney would say." Felipe tossed the gym bag to his side. "After Johnson drives back, I'm going to visit Stonehenge with Sara. It sounds corny, but there's something about her that intrigues me. *Je ne sais quoi* – her angsty eyes, perhaps. I told her that I'm glad that human eyes have no cookies, or she might find me staring at her for more than necessary. She doesn't get it, and that's what I like about her. If you delay our field trip, I might sign you up for the Bear Grylls Survival Academy. I'm sure Sidney would be happy to see you pursue another opportunity to enhance your cross-cultural competencies."

Chance ignored him and went to the bathroom.

*Later.*

"I'll come and pick you up at five." Johnson saluted him and drove off.

Chance found his way to the training ground again. Turner was busying himself with a punching bag.

"G' morning," Turner swiped his forehead. "Did the homework?"

"Hmm," Chance nodded. "I put down a few paragraphs on the way here."

Turner took off his boxing gloves, shrugged, and tied a towel around his neck. "Sidney told me that we also have a written test on the last day."

Chance sat down on an old tyre and rubbed his hands together.

*No more running today, please.*

"Slept well last night? And did you all do your homework?" Sidney walked in with a gush of wind. "Your faces tell me that you're not quite ready for the challenge today. Let's have a little warm-up run in the park for an hour to wake you up." She took off her shoulder bag and her heels and put on a pair of running shoes. "Don't give me that face, as if someone stole your scones. I'll run as well in case you think it's not fair. Come on. Time waits for no human."

An hour later, the three of them returned from their run.

The stench in the room now contained fifty-three athletes who had stayed after running a marathon.

Turner, red-faced, stood in the doorway without uttering a word while Chance gulped down a bottle of Irn-Bru.

"You can give me your homework now and take a shower." Sidney's face had not changed colour. Her students complied.

After a quick shower and a change of outfit, Chance walked out first.

Turner hummed a song in the shower.

Later, they sat on the sponge cushions, waiting for further instructions from their coach.

"Turner." Sidney held up his homework. "Good work, though a little rusty with the grammar." She held up another paper. "Then, Chance. Good structure and format, but…I don't see any emotions here. I want feelings, not just descriptions. I don't care if you saw a dog or not."

She handed back the sheets of paper and rolled a small whiteboard from the back of the room. "Now that we've had feedback on the homework. Let's start today's lesson." She used a black marker and wrote three words on it: man, monkey, and lizard.

"What do you think of these three words?" Sidney asked.

Turner raised his hand slightly. "Evolution theory, maybe."

"And the lizard?"

"Amphibians…suggesting life first came from the ocean."

"And you?" She looked at Chance.

"That well-dressed people may be beasts within," he responded, recalling the events from last night.

"Both of you touched upon the point. And, as Matthew Scudder said, I do agree that sometimes the best cloak of invisibility is a three-piece suit." Their instructor tapped the whiteboard with the marker. "Our brain is a complex organ, but in simple terms, it can be divided into three sections: humans, monkeys, and lizards. The 'human' part is the neocortex, the command control for rational thinking and decision-making. The 'monkey' part is the limbic system for emotions, while the 'lizard' part is for motor skills. In emergencies, the human will be replaced by the monkey and lizard for self-protection."

Turner took out a small notebook and wrote down their coach's words carefully.

"When we feel danger, our limbs tend to get cold. That's because the body knows it needs to protect the heart by allowing blood to flow back. It's the same when we get butterflies in our stomachs when we are nervous." She looked at her students. "Or, in the words of Jane Austen, it's simply sense and sensibility."

\* \* \*

It was almost six by the time Chance got back to his temporary residence in Oval.

He was tired out as he slumped on the settee. They had run again in the afternoon.

A long, black, open umbrella rested in the corner of the living room. He wanted to get up and close it, but in the end, he didn't move. He was not a superstitious person, at least not before Isabel's death. He remembered that they had shared a Duchesse pear only days before her accident.

*Perhaps that's why…*

A song by Lisa Ono filled the rooms as Chance picked up his thoughts.

Felipe leaned on a chair in the bedroom, "Given the right time and location, anyone could kill." He walked out of the room and showed Chance his recently read book.

Another mystery.

"This was a so-so story. Not all writers can pull off a pastiche. I hate it when *nazotoki** is in the final chapter and before dinner. I couldn't help but jump to the last few pages to find out who the murderer was," he commented. "Did you know that cyanide does not always have the 'bitter almond' smell as often told in tales? Sometimes it can be odourless. And if a suitable time is allowed, some sulphur compounds can oxidise and disappear from the human body. A coroner may not even detect it. But it'll leave signs of damage to internal organs – one plausible theory to explain what happened at Dyatlov. I'm also thoroughly tired of the cliché about hiding leaves in forests. Every writer trots out the same rhetoric. I'll bet that nine out of ten books have that phrase in them somewhere. If I were to write, the best way to hide a leaf is not in the woods. You can grind it, make a smoothie, drink it, let it out of your system, use that liquid to water the plants, then harvest the fruits, and dry it, outsource a satellite launch, and send it to space, then make it explode. The best way of deep-sixing a leaf is to hide it in the universe. Do you know what *intestate* means? So many Japanese writers like to write mysteries about resolving inheritances. I wonder how many of them really understand the rich. Before we dive into the nitty-gritty, what difference does it make if the killer was a man in a dress or a woman in pants? No, 'trousers' would be the right word around here. What difference does it make if the killer is a Scot in a kilt or an alien in a kimono? If there's no difference, why do some writers like to elaborate unnecessarily? Why do they attribute so many unfortunate events to a single garment? Because they don't take time to probe deeper? Or do they feel entitled to have a say in others' business? I once read that the cuckoo has two distinct advantages over other birds: a unique muscle on its back to throw off the other birdies from their nests and a cry that is irresistible to the foster-parent birds. A cuckoo may well fool the unknowing reed warbler, but certainly not the Marsh harrier."

Felipe smiled and handed the book to Chance. "If we all enjoyed a happy childhood with happy parents, if our neighbours, friends, and families all lived a contented life, wouldn't it be likely that prisons, barracks, and asylums would be empty? Wouldn't it be the case that the herd is kinder, the society wiser, and cosmopolitanism achieved more efficiently? Given the right time and location, anyone could kill. Not mentioning a less suitable *milieu*." He sighed. "Life is a decision tree too complex to be drawn out on paper. And a Monte Carlo simulation unworthy to be run with a handful of constraints."

Chance took the book and placed it on a side table.

Felipe continued. "I've had a very productive day. We went to Stonehenge. How should I put it? It was worth seeing but not worth paying for. A small episode happened on the way. Sara saw a travel brochure about Nara in the car, and then she was unsettled. I asked her why. She pointed out the map and asked me why were there so many swastikas and whether they represented concentration camps. Now, they wouldn't do that on a tourist-oriented pamphlet, would they? Unless, of course, it's a dark tourism package. I told her that it's called *manji* in Japanese, and it's a holy symbol that can be found in many Buddhist temples. And I told her about the prisoner-of-war camps the Japanese Imperial Army kept on their main islands, in China, in Korea, in Singapore, in India, in Myanmar, and the Philippines during World War Two. And I told her my personal favourite joke, when the Germans and the Japanese advocate for human rights, I find it more agreeable listening to Judas preaching on loyalty and devotion. It's not like that they have an unblemished track record, right? She was relieved. She thanked me for being so honest, and I told her that I could be candid when I choose to do so, but many are startled by my frankness, so I reserve it for those who matter the most to me. You've always known me well. I make no bones about discussing history. Now I wonder if I should ask her about what happened in Amritsar and the concentration camps in Kenya, you know, just to balance things out a bit. On another note, what do you want for dinner? Maybe we can go to the Tamesis Dock near Vauxhall?" Felipe's voice barely covered a rock song playing on his online radio. "Or shall we order Deliveroo? I ordered Haribo earlier."

"I'm fine with nothing."

Felipe went back to the bedroom to retrieve his phone. "Suppose this is your last supper. What would you eat?"

"Can I skip this dinner? Sleep sounds more enticing." Chance closed his eyes, and the corners of his mouth twitched.

Felipe laughed. "You'll have plenty of time after for that."

"Hand-made soup noodles would be nice," Chance reminisced.

"How about curry? That was what Joyce Peng had. Curry with codeine."

Chance did not respond.

"Just some cheap stuff from a chain store. Guess when you've had enough extravagant dining experiences, you'll settle for something rustic. Do you know what my dream last dinner is? Blinis with truffles and caviar. Irish stew. And Queen of Puddings. I read this on a menu, but I can't remember where." Felipe shrugged his shoulders. "Or, she might have used the curry to swallow the horse pills easier. I wish she'd known that there are jellies in Japan, specially designed for this purpo—"

"Ahhh! Mr Grey! Nooooo!"

A scream came from upstairs. Chance opened his eyes in a flash. Suddenly, everything in the room seemed shrouded in blue.

He bounced up from the settee, his mind spinning with Sidney's words on monkey and lizard. "What's wrong?" He asked.

"Dunno." Felipe stood quietly for a while and went back to his bedroom. "I shall still have my tea even as the world goes to hell."

Incomprehensible cries muffled the song.

Chance put on his jacket, went upstairs, and knocked on the dog lady's door. The Chihuahua had died.

\* \* \*

The third day of the Krav Maga Bootcamp was intensive. Sidney explained to them the origin and history of this technique, followed by a series of drills.

They had learnt front kicks, back kicks, side kicks and how to escape if being choked from the front, the back, and cornered. They learnt to defend themselves against long and short knives, police batons, and pistols.

Chance had sincerely hoped he would never encounter any of these situations.

During the lunch break, he chewed on the sandwich he had brought and sighed as he ate. He was tired, yes, and he was upset. He could not stop his gnawing doubts. When he informed Felipe of the dog's death last night, his expression was one of boredom.

Chance could not help but suspect that Felipe had had something to do with the canine's sudden departure.

He had seen the dead Chihuahua. There were no external injuries, no blood.

"Why such a long face? Missing someone?" The instructor's voice had startled him.

Sidney held a salad box in her hand and a Diet Coke in the other.

"I had a tattoo once." She pointed to a patch of red skin on her left arm. "A matching tattoo for couples. After I and my ex broke up, it took many laser sessions to remove it. Guess it served me well." She laughed bitterly. "A wound on the skin might heal easily, not so easily deep inside. You know, when I was a kid, we used to fool around with something we called an 'Indian burn'. It's the feeling you get when you twist someone's wrists. Sadness does burn."

Chance, still chewing on the sandwich, bit his cheek inside.

Sidney opened her salad box. "I meant to ask you something. Are you left-handed? You wear your watch on your right hand, but I think your usual hand is the right."

"No. I just like to wear it that way."

He recalled Joyce Peng's diary entry on watches and nail polishes.

And her last dinner was curry and codeine.

"Have you ever been hospitalised?"

"Yes." He admitted less willingly. "I had an accident once. A motorcycle jumped the light. I was crossing the road. I thought it would stop, but it didn't."

Sidney nodded while picking at her mealy salad. "We should exercise more. That'll do us favours." She looked down at her wrists. "Look at these bones. Don't they resemble sticks of rhubarb? But they are very strong. I'd say that life's a sport."

"Hey! Listen! I did it!" Turner trotted around the corner, puffing and blowing. His face was glowing like a waxed apple. "Just now, a bilker refused to pay his cab fare, and I subdued him using the elbow strike we learnt today! Guess I know a way or two to deal with difficult customers!"

"What happened to the man? We better take him to the police."

"The cabbie was kind enough, and she didn't want to waste no time." Turner swiped his forehead. "We let him leave once he paid. He was dressed up all smart. Who'd know?"

Sidney swallowed a cucumber slice. "How's the pub going?"

"Pretty well. We're applying for loans. It can be a bit tricky; sometimes, the computer says no." Turner gave a confident smile. "When we open, you two are welcome, twenty per cent discount."

"Good to know." Sidney laughed. "However, there are times when the smoother things go, the more suspicious you have to be." She put down her plastic fork. "I have a friend who's into self-defence training. He'd heard there's a bodyguard academy in Dubai. The graduates there worked for the riches in the Middle East and could afford a Porsche within a year of their graduation. He went there, paid a lot of money in tuition, graduated, and couldn't find one single decent job. It turned out that the academy hired a Porsche and had someone drive around campus in it, so more students were lured into the trap. Guess the lesson is that all that seems well does not necessarily mean all is well."

Sidney laughed boldly again. "Another guy I know lied about his CV. He claimed that he was ex-SAS, then he was recruited as a bodyguard for an envoy in Iraq. He ended up misfiring his gun at his VIP because he was not familiar with the weapons at all." She looked at Chance. "So, my advice is to listen attentively and doubt everything."

"Yep, we better keep our eyes and ears open," Turner reflected.

"Since you have finished eating–" Sidney eyed her students– "why don't you go for a run in the park? The weather's lovely today."

\* \* \*

Dinner was at Big & Easy in Covent Garden.

Chance walked into the barbecue and seafood restaurant. A Sinatra song, unknown to him, was playing.

Saturday evening gathered quite a crowd.

Felipe was sitting by the counter hugging a milkshake. A waiter was standing on a ladder, trying to retrieve a bottle of whiskey stored high on a shelf.

"I don't understand the culinary landscape in London," Felipe said dryly. "Japanese restaurants owned by Koreans, Korean restaurants owned by the British, and Chinese restaurants owned by the French. It's comforting to know that the American joints are still owned by the Americans. Not that I'm against the waves of glocalisation," he frowned, "but it does raise doubts as to the authenticity of the food here in London. You know me, I'm pedantic about dining."

"Johnson told me that you went to a Nikkei restaurant for lunch. Did it not reach your standards?"

Felipe did not reply. He finished his milkshake and gestured to a waiter to take them to their reserved table.

A child on a neighbouring table was sharing her excitement about a coding summer school she hoped to attend and how she aspired to become the next Zuckerberg.

"All restaurants should have a smoking zone and a kid-free zone. What do you think of the common trope whereby adults tell children that they can become anyone they want to be?" Felipe asked, casually browsing the menu.

Chance recalled his childhood. "Sometimes, some encouragement would do them good."

"What if the children say that they want to become a murderer; a terrorist, even?" Felipe put down the menu and sighed. "Perhaps it's equally important to tell them that they do not need to become whoever they want to be, and they certainly can't become whoever they want to be. Do you know what I didn't learn at HBS? Just because you can do something doesn't mean you should do it. Ninety-nine per cent of managers in the IT industry wants to become the next Bill Gates, and they all end up as Bill Sikes."

Someone dropped a fork in the distance.

Chance collected his thoughts. "Circumstances could limit one's options."

"I read somewhere that Superman is a great teacher of class consciousness because he stands for justice, and there's no justice under capitalism. I'd say you don't have justice in socialism nor autocracy, democracy, and mediocracy

– excellent food for thought. You'd be surprised how TV and mass media affect people's mentality. Do you know that the Astro Boy and his sister Uran were designed to brainwash the Japanese population so they wouldn't resist plans for building nuclear power stations in the 1950s and 60s? And *Godzilla* came from fear of nuclear contamination." Felipe picked up the menu again. "Tell me about your day. More running? I might need to discuss with Sidney if the fees are too high for a course made up mostly of running."

"We learnt a lot today. I brought three T-shirts, and now they smell like brine."

"Can't say that our client's money went to waste now." Felipe nodded approvingly. "Have you heard that everything can be solved with salt water? Sweat and persevere when you're in trouble, cry when you can't, and once you have exhausted all your tricks, find a *misaki** near the sea. One jump will do." He stared at Chance. "I have a feeling that you're not the type to attempt suicide."

Chance smiled faintly. "I'm not sure if I should take that as a compliment. I guess…I'm either too stubborn or too scared."

"Scudder? Good point." Felipe looked around and fixed his eyes on a neon sign glittering the restaurant's name. "For some, a big decision is an easy one to make." He turned back. "So, the Bootcamp ends tomorrow, right?"

Chance took a deep breath. "We'll have a test in the morning. A written one to detail what techniques to implement in what situation."

"As Joyce Peng's diary said, teachers are always conflicted." Felipe shrugged. "On the one hand, the questions have to be difficult to be a true measure of a gauge of the students' abilities. On the other hand, teachers also want their protégés to do well. So good luck to you." He knocked twice on the heavy wood table and looked up at the small blackboard hanging on the ceiling. "I think I'll have lobster."

A waiter came to take their order.

Chance decided on a lobster roll and a lemonade.

After their food arrived, Felipe kept on talking. "They often speculate about the first crab eater. I do wonder what happened to the first lobster eater. Must have been quite a courageous act."

"Perhaps someone who's very poor," Chance inspected his surroundings. "In the 17th and 18th centuries, only the poor ate lobster. For those in service, their contracts would specify that lobster was served no more than twice a week, or else they would consider the working conditions to be bad. Rich families ate meat."

Felipe laughed. "Do you know the other name for lobster?"

Chance nodded.

"Then better not to say it, in case we lose our appetites."

\* \* \*

*An hour later.*

Felipe asked for the bill and added a large tip. "Tip generously, unless you don't plan on coming back," he commented. "I was a waiter once as well."

Chance stood at Felipe's side, looking at a wall decorated with business cards, remembering how happy Isabel had been when she showed him her first business card after securing an internship at a law firm.

They left the restaurant; it was balmy outside.

Chance took off his jacket and draped it over his shoulder as they walked to the Strand.

"Johnson took me to Whitechapel today. Isn't it a rose by another name? It didn't look very white; I have to say. The collars, I mean. Oh! And we went to the Cereal Killer Cafe! Did you know that there's a boutique consultancy in London called Autopsy that specialises in analysing failed start-ups? Catchy names these are. Did you know how Jeffrey Dahmer differed from most serial killers? He killed outside his own ethnicity. Hey, hey, things are complicated in these countries with no capital punishment. Dennis Nilsen is still rotting away in prison. Prisons are a great social platform for criminals to get together to learn new trades and how to steal and kill with fewer years if caught again. Hell, some rooms in private prisons in the US even beat college accommodation in Japan. Johnson also entertained me with some Victorian folklore: Jack the Ripper, Spring-Heeled Jack. I wonder why all the bad-ass boys were named Jack. This reminds me that I once heard an urban legend–" Felipe lit a cigarette– "that in our not-so-small world of investment banking, there's a company with an arcane division known to a few as MIS, which stands for 'Mercenaries in Suits'. Urban legend has it that they operate from China to Peru–" he took a drag– "and once I met an opposite number from there over some dealings. As curious as my nature is, I couldn't help but ask him if the rumours were true. If indeed they used code names for their dodgy business. For example, a 'merger' meant murder, and an 'acquisition' meant an abduction. He only grinned at me and said, 'Felipe, rest assured. The professionals never develop Lima Syndrome'."

It mizzled as they walked.

Felipe turned to him. "The rain in Spain falls mainly on the plain. The former King of Spain goes mostly to his plane. I've been inside a Lockheed Jetstar once, and it made me claustrophobic. It's good to know that Covent

Garden still looks like the set of *My Fair Lady*. I wonder where the acid rain in the UK falls mainly."

Someone afar played 'Scarborough Fair' on the violin.

Chance licked the wound where he had bitten his mouth.

Isabel used to make him say a tongue twister in Spanish. It was about three sad tigers.

*Sadness indeed burns.*

Felipe stopped as they passed a chain sushi place. He smoked as he peeped into the store. "Yesterday, I happened to run into someone who grows wasabi. He told me that only one per cent of the wasabi is natural in the chain stores across the UK. The rest is artificial or mustard. I dare say that I have found a good business opportunity."

"I believe it's a common practice to cut costs," Chance said while distracted. He was still thinking about the three tigers.

Felipe extinguished his cigarette on his shoe sole. "They say that every cigarette will make you live for ten minutes less. But every day I spend working will shorten my life span by several hours. Smoking certainly beats working."

They followed the chiaroscuro of cobbled streets and didn't speak on the way back.

*** 

*The next day.*

After Chance and Turner had submitted their written paper, Sidney stood in front of her students.

"This concludes our four-day intensive Krav Maga Bootcamp. I hope that you've learnt what you came to learn and what you hoped to learn." She watched them like an old cat watching kittens. "Now, I want to share three pieces of advice with you. They've been handy in my life so far, and I hope they will do you two good as well." She crossed her arms and cleared her throat, "My first piece of advice is that no matter the location or timing, be it in a downtown area or on a country road, don't stare at others. Eye contact can be interpreted as provocative. Watch where you're going, watch the sky, but don't watch the others."

They nodded.

"My second point is don't provoke. Don't use self-defence techniques unless you *absolutely* have to. Let's say you're walking down the street, and you see a fight taking place. Do you go up and confront them, or do you run away?" She laughed. "Always run away. Never put yourself in a dangerous situation unless it is absolutely, one thousand per cent necessary."

She smiled shyly. "The last is practical advice. When you travel, or even in everyday life, prepare a second wallet. Get a second-hand one from Oxfam and stuff it with newspaper cuttings. If you ever get mugged, throw this fake wallet as far away as you can. Then run. It could buy you some time."

"What if…" Turner asked, "what if they put a knife to my neck and told me to retrieve the fake. Wouldn't they be livid if they found out?"

"Well." Sidney thought. "Rule number one is never to put yourself in a dangerous position." She stepped forward and tapped on the whiteboard. "I've said all that I wanted to say. The rest is to say goodbye and good luck to you. The test will not be scored; it's just for reference. I'll send out some files over email later. And don't forget to practise and exercise. Learning without practising is like learning in vain."

They shook hands.

"I wish you all the best with the pub," Sidney said to Turner. "I'm counting on the discount."

Chance parted with Turner after saying goodbye. Johnson brought him back to Oval.

It was almost three by the time he got back. He took off his coat and hung it on a hook behind the door. The air was stuffy, so he opened the windows.

Felipe was in the bedroom, whispering something, perhaps taking a call. His leather sap rested on the settee, next to a small, upended cardboard box the size of a phone.

Chance picked up the leather sap and weighed it in his hand.

*This could hurt a lot*, he thought as he recalled their night out a few days ago.

He wondered if Felipe had used the sap on the dog.

He sat on the settee; the lady upstairs still whined occasionally from Mr Grey's passing.

Chance put down the sap as soon as he saw the bedroom door open. He then walked into the kitchen, took out a glass, turned on the tap, and filled it.

"Only drink tap water if you wish to have a balding head," Felipe joked. "I know quicker ways to achieve your desired hairstyle. At least get a Brita." Felipe opened the fridge and dug out a Corona. "Training's over? I hope you didn't spend our client's money in vain. Mercury has great perks, even Netflix membership." He downed the beer. "Johnson told me that, since last year, the UK's Office for National Statistics had added Netflix to their basket of goods. I'm following *Hannibal*, the TV show, on there."

"I don't watch Netflix."

"No, you don't. I sometimes wonder if you watch anything or pay attention to anything at all." Felipe put down the empty beer bottle.

"Tomorrow's Monday. You should start adding value as well. I've arranged for you to meet Catherine. Afterwards, we'll pay a short visit to Joyce Peng's apartment. No need to sweat; the room's been thoroughly cleaned. If you still have doubts, bring some salt*."

Felipe retrieved his leather sap and tucked it under his shirt. "You can ask Catherine about her stalker." He smiled mysteriously. "I hope you two have a pleasant meeting. And I almost forgot…" He picked up the small cardboard box on the settee, opened it, and took out a black, flashlight-like object. "This is for you. Just in case."

Chance held up the flashlight. "I'm not sure if it's legal to carry a taser around here."

"I'm not asking you to harm peaceful and honest citizens like me, am I? Use it on bad people and in emergencies only," Felipe explained. "Can I place my trust in you that she will not be hurt?"

"I have said this before, and I will repeat it. I'm not the best choice as a bodyguard." Chance hesitated. "You certainly have more experience in combat than I do. "

"Do you know what your problem is? You are a 'yes but-ter'. I'm a 'why not-ter'. Never use the word 'but', and never say 'never' – by the way, that's a song. Stop using words that are forbidden in the IDEO repertoire. One of them being 'I can't'. Why don't you change it to 'how might we?' How might we solve this problem for the client? Try to picture this in your head. The night before your wedding, you find out that your fiancé has been cheating, and more than once, with more than one person. The wedding is cancelled, and you decide to spend some time far away from home to reconcile with this ugly fact. Now, you have calmed your feelings, and you are back in London, only to find that someone tries to break into your kitchen the very morning you get back. How unsettling all this is!" Felipe exclaimed. "Could you not show some support to our friend here?"

Chance sighed.

"And do me a favour: don't try to take advantage of the situation," Felipe said sternly. "That I simply will not allow."

Chance nodded as he noticed a cockroach crawling across the floor. He moved quickly and trapped it under the cardboard box.

"Well…" He let out a sigh of relief. "Help me get the insecticide in your room? It's in the bag Johnson brought yesterday from Robert Dyas."

Felipe didn't budge but looked sheepishly at him. "We already had our fair share of lobsters; why don't we spare their brother on the land?"

There was a sudden wave of shouting downstairs.

Chance kept the cardboard box where it was and went out to investigate.

The lady upstairs had sent Mr Grey for a necropsy, and the results showed that the Chihuahua had died of chocolate poisoning. A neighbour's child admitted his wrongdoing. He hadn't liked his chocolate Easter bunny.

# CHAPTER 5

**13**th April was a sunny day.

Chance got into the Rover's front seat, fastened his seat belt, and listened to the morning radio as Johnson drove.

Eight o'clock on a Monday morning was a headache for many. People passed in all directions, carrying to-go cups of various sizes, backpacks, handbags, and suitcases, heading to their respective workplaces and schools.

For some, today, like yesterday and the day before, would be another monotonous cycle of twenty-four hours. For others, today would be memorable. Some would be scolded, and some would lose their jobs, some would get married, some would file for divorce, some would be glad that they were still alive, others would be troubled that they were not dead yet.

"Mr Kazama wants you to meet him in front of the Aldwych Theatre at ten," Johnson said as they waited for a light. "It's not far from the Temple Garden."

"Thank you. I'm somewhat familiar with this area."

"Good to know." The young driver stroked his chin. "Message me if there's any problem. And how was your Krav Maga course?" He asked nervously. "I've chatted with Turner. He told me he's planning to open a pub." He laughed like a horse. "London lacks many things. Heathrow lacks a runway. The Underground lacks staff, and the whole city could do with more sunshine. The only thing it does not lack is pubs. He might be better off selling fridges to the Eskimos or sand to the Sahara…or coals to Newcastle." He showed his shell-like teeth.

The light went green, and their car dashed off like a dog chasing a cat. Crowds of tourists had gathered in Trafalgar Square, waiting for the National Gallery to open. Some children were trying to climb onto the statues of black lions, and pigeons flew low.

"Eh…" Johnson shook his head and sighed. "Traffic here is terrible."

"Perhaps you could pull over?" Chance suggested. "I might as well walk; it's not far anyway."

"There's no need. We're only a short distance from our destination." Johnson laughed timidly. "Mr Kazama made me promise that I would take you there in case you…missed the early meeting. It must be quite tough."

"As in?"

"Working under…*with* Mr Kazama," Johnson mused. "My boss told me only to believe a third of what Felipe Kazama has to say because he keeps a third to himself and eats another third for his stomach."

Chance did not comment.

A helicopter roamed high above.

Johnson winced. "There's an article in *The Guardian* earlier about a police helicopter unit in London abusing Twitter commenters who complained about the noise." He shook his head. "The last time I saw one was when they filmed *London Has Fallen* near Aldwych. Now there's a fire, and they're doing all this work for a show."

Johnson manoeuvred the car forward slowly and finally stopped beside the road shoulder. "You can enter here." He pointed to a riveted iron gate next to a café on the right. "Go in and go straight. Just tell the receptionist that you have an appointment with barrister Cecil Stone. Call me if you need anything."

"Thank you."

Chance got out of the car and walked toward Pump Court.

Cecil Stone was a portly, stern-looking barrister with a balding head. He had a white silk shirt and a diamond-patterned wool vest. A silver ring decorated his left ring finger, and a pair of gold-rimmed spectacles sat on his nose.

His office had a simple layout. A few commendations garnished the wall by the glass bookshelves. A mahogany desk hosted a phone, a desktop computer, three photos, and a dozen folders. Behind the desk was a matching swivel chair. Behind the chair was a large-framed window where Chance saw a plane crossing the sky.

"Mr Yang? I'm glad that you're here." Cecil Stone got up from his chair and reached out his hand. "I was afraid that Felipe had forgotten all about me and my...nodus."

"I'd like to meet with Miss Catherine Roxborough as soon as possible to discuss how I might be of assistance."

The barrister looked at his watch. "She should be here soon."

Suddenly, the desk phone rang.

"Give me a moment, please." The barrister picked it up and whispered, "Yes, I'm on my way." He grabbed a folder from his desk. "Be right there."

Cecil Stone ended the call and looked around. "I had a broken guest chair, and we're in the process of replacing it. Why don't you sit down for a while and wait in here?" He patted the arm of the swivel chair next to him.

"Please don't be concerned," Chance offered. "I'll wait in the visitors' room."

"Please, I insist." The barrister smiled. "I trust Felipe, and I trust you."

"Then I will respectfully oblige," Chance answered politely.

"I'm sure she'll be here any minute," Cecil Stone said before leaving the room.

Chance stood for a while and finally decided to take the only seat.

All the running had made his back sore.

He examined the objects on the desk. The desktop had the default screensaver for Windows. Two photo frames showed Cecil and a woman of his age, presumably his wife or sister. Another featured the barrister and the Queen.

He turned back in his chair to look out of the window. Clouds drifted from east to west like a migrating flock of sheep.

Isabel had loved cloud watching.

He remembered a Greek myth she had told him. A story about the cloud nymph, Nephele, a young woman who always carried a jar in her arms as she moved around in the sky, sprinkling the world with water.

Isabel had gone like a cloud.

So quick, as if to leave no trace behind.

What if he had accompanied her to that law ball on that night?

If and only if.

* * *

Catherine had not been well lately. The admin post that her godfather had in mind for her was very dull indeed. Not only did she have to deal with paper-pushing, but the work also required all female staff to wear high heels, meaning that she limped back home every day.

By the time she got to Temple Underground Station, she was five minutes away from running late. She pushed her way through the crowd, ran up the stairs, and beeped her card out.

It was sunny outside. She managed to put on her sunglasses.

She hated work. No, she hated the job that Cecil had got her.

*Monday work. Mundane work.*

*Mondayitis…Make it weekdayitis…*

Discussions on nepotism were a common theme during office tea breaks. She knew very well at whom these comments were directed, and she couldn't help but notice them.

Life was bad.

Life was bad, indeed.

*Three minutes to go.*

She looked at her watch, bypassing the garden gate, and took a shortcut into the Pump Court.

Catherine made it on time by the skin of her teeth.

"Mr Stone is waiting for you in his office. Please hurry," Souhini shot her a strange look as she wobbled her head.

Catherine muttered her thanks and trotted upstairs.

She had lasted a week. She marvelled at how she'd been able to stay for so long.

*Perhaps this is the right time to tell Cecil.*

Catherine decided that she would leave the job. Even Sophie had encouraged her, during their weekend reunion, to find a career that she truly loved, rather than obeying whatever plans Cecil and her uncle had in store.

Yes, Catherine thought.

*I will do it. I will do it now.*

She took off her sunglasses, held them in her hands, knocked on the door lightly, took a deep breath, and entered.

Cecil was sitting in his swivel chair, thinking with his back to her.

*Just handy.*

She was not sure if she could speak up if they were face to face.

Upon hearing the door opening, he wanted to turn around, but not before he heard someone saying, "Please don't turn around. I have something important to say. And please don't say anything. Not until I have finished my part."

Whoever had come into the office must have mistaken him for the owner.

"Cecil, I know that you care for me deeply and have my best interests at heart, which is why you have arranged this job for me, but I don't think that I'm a suitable candidate. I've no legal background, and I'm not interested in furthering myself in the field. I have my life plans, and I'm not…"

*How many people laid well-made plans but never had the chance to follow up on them? Some were too lazy; some had no resources and connections; some had no time nor…life to do it,* he thought.

"You might think that I'm not ambitious," the voice continued. "I cannot say that this job has tickled my fancy. But you have to trust me. Alex has to trust me as well. Pierre is history, and now, all I want is to have some time to do what I enjoy doing, like writing, like designing. I have decided to leave the Chamber today, and I have made up my mind."

Catherine was surprised at how fast she could talk.

Cecil sat still.

*He must be disappointed now.*

She swallowed, waiting for her ordeal.

"If you have nothing else to say, I will head out and prepare my handover."

A pause.

Catherine watched as the clouds drifted away.

"I am afraid that I have no authority over this issue."

All of a sudden, a slight American accent seeped in.

The chair turned; a man was sitting in it.

Not Cecil.

Not someone she had recognised.

He was Asian, medium build, on the thin side.

*Oh no*, Catherine thought as he stood up and walked over to her side of the table.

"Good morning, Miss Roxborough. I am truly sorry for the misunderstanding." He gestured towards the chair. "Mr Stone insisted that I use his chair while… Well… Now that you're here, we can discuss…"

"Where is Cecil, and who are you exactly?"

He looked a little bit surprised. "Mr Stone was called away to a meeting. My name is Changxi Yang. I'm here to assist you."

"I certainly do not need your assistance in any matter."

"Mr Stone told me that you had an unfortunate encounter with a suspicious individual who tried to break into your house. I could help you to set up a CCTV system around your premises."

*This is all getting out of hand.*

"Mister…I do not need a CCTV system; I do not need your assistance. What I need is for you to tell Cecil that he has no right to meddle with my life!"

Catherine clutched her sunglasses tightly.

*Umm.* Chance recalled. When was the last time that he was confronted like this?

The man looked at her, then thought for a few seconds. "Very well. If that is what you wish, I will tell him." He paused. "Do you want me to pass on your resignation as well?"

"No. That won't be necessary."

"I see." The man nodded. "Miss Roxborough, since the weather is very nice today, might I suggest that you reconfigure your sunglasses? They seem to be…"

Catherine looked down. A lens was missing.

\* \* \*

*Later.*

When Chance appeared at the intersection, Felipe checked his watch. Nine fifty-five sharp.

*Early as usual.*

"I hope you didn't pose any difficulties for her."

"There has been a little misunderstanding. She has expressed that she doesn't need any assistance from me."

"Well. We've got no time to grieve for roses when the forests are burning. You didn't want to be the bodyguard, and now it seems that you no longer have to. Let's go and ring a ring of roses." Felipe led the way. "We might as well finish the task at hand and have a long vacation."

They walked up Drury Lane and turned onto Kean Street. A woman in a charcoal dress suit was making a phone call in front of a large double glass door. A few office workers were smoking and chatting near the entrance.

"I'll need some time here. Now, how can you get the date on the deed of surrender wrong? Listen, I've got to go…" They heard the estate agent dishing out as they approached her.

She finished her call and hurriedly dropped her phone into her briefcase.

"You must be Felipe Kazama. I'm Enid Abara from NP Properties."

They shook hands and introduced each other.

"Gentlemen," Enid hesitated, "I have some urgent matters waiting back in the office…"

"In that case," Felipe suggested, "why don't you leave the keys with us? We won't delay you."

Enid looked at Felipe questioningly. "That would be against protocols."

"Then I'd ask you to accompany us – only a few questions. Won't be long," Felipe said as his phone rang. "Now, if you'll excuse me, I have to take this call." He gestured to Chance. "Why don't you two go upstairs first?"

The estate agent took out a white key card from her briefcase and tapped it onto the card reader by the door.

"Please follow me." She walked to the lift as the Asian man followed.

*Chance. What a strange name. Like the name of a fixer from an old Western film.* She thought as she called down the lift.

"Miss Abara, did you ever meet Joyce Peng?" The man asked as they waited.

"Yes. Only once, though."

"Was it on the day before…"

"Yes. The day before she…passed away."

The lift came; they walked in. There was a large mirror inside.

"Was that the afternoon of 5th April?"

"Yes," Enid recalled. "Because of the fire, I was asked to do a round of fire and safety checks at the apartments. I saw her coming out of her apartment, and I asked her to complete a survey on the problems that she had experienced. You know, the utilities, if they were functioning or not."

"And how was she faring at that time?"

Enid thought for a moment. "She was quite normal. Maybe she was a bit moody; I couldn't say for certain. Her nose was red and running. I asked her if everything was alright, and she told me that she had a bad hay fever. I suggested to her that wearing a mask might help. My sister-in-law lives in Japan, and she has a terrible pollen allergy. She told me that she had one on her and was going to wear it outside."

"Ninth floor," a synthesised female voice announced.

They left the lift.

"Anything else you remember?"

"Nothing particularly noteworthy." Enid raised her head as she tried to recall. "When she called my colleague David on the day of the fire, she gave him a new number. He wished me to confirm with her whether we should update her contact details."

"Yes, and?"

"She told me to update her details," Enid opened a wooden door. A quiet atrium surrounded by lush vegetation hid behind it. They went through the door.

He thanked her as they stopped in front of apartment five.

"Come to think about it, there's one thing she said that gave me the creeps," Enid admitted.

He waited.

"As we came out of the lift, she told me that it seemed a fine day for some curry."

Chance pondered for a moment and heard the estate agent's phone ringing again. She excused herself from taking the call.

*A minute later.*

"Look, Mr Yang, if you have no more questions, I must get going. My superior has agreed to leave the keys here. Please return them to the front desk once you are finished. She told me that you might need them for several days. To reach the front desk, you will need to go to the main entrance on Kingsway," Enid explained as she handed him a ring of keys and the white key card.

"We'll do that. Thank you," Chance replied.

Enid hurried towards the lift, just as Felipe stepped out, talking on his Jabra wireless earphone.

"A change of scenery could do them good. Everybody knows that the pollution in Central London is way worse. And good planning certainly takes time. Ah! This poor signal. The Voyager 1 could do a better job." He ended his call on his Jabra and gave Enid a wide smile. "Miss Abara, Enid, could you enlighten me on an issue?"

"Y...yes?"

"Which telecom company do you use, and, on a scale of zero to ten, considering your user experience, how likely are you to recommend it to a friend or family?"

*That's a way to ask a question.*

"I'm with Three. I like it, and it's quite okay for me. It depends on your needs. If you need more calling time or more data, I've heard...perhaps I saw it on the Underground...There's a place that offers a 'buy one get one free' scheme. You can get a twin card for your tablet if you have one."

"My needs...Very well. 'Buy one get one free' does sound like a rather enticing offer. I might look into it then decide whether to switch," Felipe smiled. "Have a nice day."

\* \* \*

When Chance entered Joyce Peng's apartment, the first thing he noticed was the scramble of footsteps on the white marble tiles in the vestibule.

The air was stale, like an intact tomb. For a moment, he wondered if he should light a candle to test if there was enough oxygen in there like a tomb robber would.

He ventured into the room with his shoes on, examined the various pieces of furniture covered by white sheets, then found his way upstairs.

The bedroom curtains were drawn. A sliver of light shone through the slit.

He pressed a switch on the wall, and a crystal ceiling light illuminated the room.

The bed where Joyce Peng last lay had been cleaned.

*Waiting for its next dreamer, perhaps.*

A dressing table with bottles of organic skincare products and jars of everyday amenities, including a liquid bandage, stood next to two white wardrobes.

He opened a wardrobe. Several belts hung like dead snakes. One had a small, orange inscription on the inside: if you cannot be faithful to your own individuality, you cannot be loyal to anything.

He had recognised the logo from a leather goods shop on Long Acre.

The study had boxes of books on the floor. He didn't bother to open them. There was a novel by Paulo Coelho on the desk, *Veronika Decides to Die*, a MacBook, and a white Epson printer. He recalled the content of its last printout.

*This is not goodbye.*

A picture showed Joyce Peng and another young woman together. They were of similar height.

Small sounds of hard disk operating came. He tapped the laptop's touchpad, but the screen did not respond.

One heavy book hid behind the printer. It was on suicide by someone called Durkheim. The book had a white patch taped onto its spine, marking it the property of a nearby university library.

*Perhaps it might be worthwhile checking her borrowing records.*

Felipe came into the study. "Johnson has arranged for you to speak with the ex this afternoon. Five fifteen. You can meet her at the pharmacy when her shift is over." He looked around and flipped through a few pages of the book on suicide. "I think I'll leave you to yourself for the afternoon. I'm sure you don't need me to accompany you to your music teacher. I will check out J. M. W. Turner's blue plaque in Maiden Lane to enhance my cross-cultural competency. Oh...and remember to use the Columbo technique."

*Later.*

After chicken soup and a croissant for lunch, Chance followed the directions on his phone and found the entrance to the Actors' Centre, a multi-purpose building in Soho. Several actors in costumes had lined up in front of the reception desk. He waited for his turn and asked for the whereabouts of the room for vocal training.

A lady led him through a metal corridor and then instated him in front of a black door.

A group sat on a long, old couch in the lounge area, talking about their most recent auditions.

He looked at his watch: five to two. There were some leaflets and advertisements on the wall beside him. He stood there and read them.

A voice came behind him, neither coarse nor weak. "Are you here for the singing taster?"

He turned. "Yes. I only signed up last night… A little late."

"Well, nothing is too late." The owner of the voice smiled. "I'm in charge of today's course. Just call me Sam."

Sam wore a white blouse, ankle-length skirt and straw sandals, with a Cath Kidston lunch bag in hand. "How did you hear about us?" Sam asked. "We hope to enhance our outreach efforts at the City Academy."

He hesitated before answering. "A friend had been on a taster course before. So, I wanted to give it a try…" He paused. "She attended the course two weeks ago."

"Oh! I was here as well," Sam marvelled. "We had a girl who's so good at the tongue twisters. Better than I did even."

"Tongue twisters?"

"Yeah," Sam nodded. "We do a lot of tongue twisters in our taster session. Like, 'unique New York', 'Seth at Sainsbury's sells thick socks', and 'red lorry, yellow lorry' to warm up. That girl, Joyce, she's so good at them."

He hesitated again. "Ah. Joyce. She's the friend I was talking about."

"I thought so," Sam blinked. "I remembered her because she has the same name as my sister. So how is she faring? Is she coming back for a full term of lessons?"

"I am afraid that she's rather…busy for now."

"Well…all the same." Sam gave a heavy sigh. "That's why we might want to make time for hobbies."

He nodded and noticed that a small item had fallen out of Sam's lunch bag. He stooped down and picked it up. It was a heart-shaped picture.

"Oops." Sam retrieved it quickly. "I'm making a scrapbook for my honey to celebrate our anniversary. A secret project during my lunch breaks."

They talked a bit more then he listened as Sam recounted their trip to Guilin the year before.

\* \* \*

The taster session passed quickly. Afterwards, he bought a bottle of mineral water at a roadside stall.

All the tongue twisters had made his cheeks sore.

He checked the time. Four-thirty.

He walked down Tower Street and turned left into Slingsby Place.

The small piazza had three long benches on grey bricked grounds with three restaurants garnishing its corners. A high-end home décor store and a florist completed the scene. Baskets of flowers, some unknown to him, greeted him. There were beautiful calla lilies.

He stood there and took in his surroundings. A small blackboard stood in front of the flower boutique:

*Registration opens for The Introduction to Floristry Short Course!*
*Gift Card Available!*

A couple sat on one of the benches making out.

He sighed and left.

He followed Long Acre and turned into Drury Lane for another three or four minutes, took a right and found his way to Holborn Station.

Ten or fifteen minutes later, he walked into a pharmacy. It was a small one that sold sandwiches and umbrellas as well. A few customers queued for their prescriptions; most waited for self-checkout. There was a photo booth in a corner.

He approached the medicine counter, where a woman in a lab coat stood. "Excuse me, are you Mrs Tilly Wurman?"

She looked at him. "Yes. What can I do for you?"

"I believe my colleague contacted you earlier." He paused. "Regarding… Miss Joyce Peng."

Tilly Wurman looked around. "I'm sorry. My shift isn't over yet. Perhaps you could wait outside? Or try to make yourself look busy with the products."

He nodded.

He toured the shop. Plasters were on sale, and so were energy bars. He didn't buy anything.

Tilly joined him after her shift ended. She was wearing a purple shirt and wide-legged black trousers. The cowhide shoulder bag she was carrying reminded him faintly of a butcher's apron he had once seen as a boy.

Chance introduced himself again, and they shook hands.

Her hands were cold.

Chance faltered. "Er…If…if you don't want to go to the apartment, I understand. We can find a café nearby."

Tilly looked down. "No, no. It's fine. I've passed through the stages of grief and have reached acceptance."

They walked back to the apartment.

Before entering the lobby, Tilly's phone rang. She excused herself and answered.

"Yes. Martin? I'll be a little late tonight…no…Yeah…next week? What's all this hurry?" She glanced at Chance. "Well, this is no good time to discuss…we'll talk at home. Okay, bye."

"Sorry." She put her phone down. "I need to make another quick call."

"Take your time."

Tilly called again, but her mother did not pick up, so she left a message. Chance showed her the way in; they took the lift to floor nine.

"You called Miss Peng on the morning before she…on the 5th. Do you mind me asking what you discussed?"

"Nothing serious." Tilly furrowed her brows as she recalled. "Making sure the flat was alright."

"Then on the next morning, you called her fifteen times."

Tilly nodded slowly. "I had a bad feeling. And I hated it. I had a terrible headache that day, so I tried to find some painkillers. I looked all over the house and couldn't find the codeine tablets. I was worried that Joyce might have taken them."

They passed through the atrium, and he hesitated before opening the door.

"After she didn't respond, you came over and used the spare key to open the door?"

"Yes. To check on her. I came directly from my house. Didn't even phone in at the pharmacy." Tilly nodded slightly. "We all make a habit of hiding spare keys under our doormats," she added. "The poor cleaning lady. She had such a shock."

She entered the room and pulled the curtains open. Through a giant French window, they could see people taking their tea on the rooftop of the building opposite. Children capered about on a piece of artificial grass on the rooftop.

"Some things are hard to accept but have to be accepted," Tilly mused. "We had some great times and some not-so-great times. Joyce always told me that she had hated her boarding school days. She'd call home every night. They would promise to pick her up the next morning, but they never did. Her favourite film was *Rebel Without a Cause*. I asked her why people would bite combs? It hurts their teeth, and it's very unhygienic."

*At least she said goodbye*, he thought.

He looked out of the window. "The BT Tower looks quite weird from up here."

Tilly gave a faint smile. "Quite brutal, isn't it?"

"I'm sorry?"

She pointed to a cylindrical building to the right of the window. "The Space House is another signature brutalist building. Its main feature is the exposed steel structure. The BT Tower had its round shape because the designers referred to the surviving buildings in Hiroshima and Nagasaki after the atomic bombing: the round ones were most resistant to the nuclear blast. Or so I've heard."

"Ah. Very knowledgeable about architecture." He added, "Learning from your father, I believe?"

"Yes." Tilly looked out of the window again. "Joyce used to love the view from this window. She said that you could hardly find any traces of disturbances, only busy people, birds, and clouds."

*Yes, gone like the clouds.*

He cleared his thoughts. "Did she take the plastic bag from your house as well?"

A seagull tap danced on the balcony.

"That was very silly of me," Tilly sighed. "I should have known better. I should have known when she talked about codeine and plastic bags for the first time. Huh. Silly Tilly indeed." She shook her head in regret.

"And on the first night of her stay, did she bring anything else besides the champagne?"

"No. The champagne…that's all. She didn't even have her medication or her phone charger."

"Nothing else?"

"Nothing."

Chance opened the window; urban sounds flushed in and surrounded them. He thought for a few seconds. "I've seen her credit card history. On the night of 1st April, she bought a bouquet of white roses from a florist in Slingsby Place."

# CHAPTER 6

The first time he met Isabel was at The Horseshoe at Clerkenwell. His roommate Kruz had organised a pub quiz, and he had been 'strongly advised' to come along.

It was a night of Fulham vs West Ham. He wasn't interested in the match nor the quiz. As soon as the knees-up finished, he excused himself, grabbed his jacket, and headed out.

The air outside was as cold and refreshing as a mint.

Then he heard someone shouting. "Get your hands off me, you bloody bastard!"

He looked ahead and saw two figures entangled under the pale streetlight.

"Isabel, now, listen to me," a man's voice pleaded. "For one minute, please!"

"I don't want anything from you. Let me go." The woman returned coldly.

"Let me explain. We were...it was...I...I'm so very sorry..."

"You should be!"

"I...I didn't...I didn't know. I did not know that you...that she..." the man struggled. "Please! I hope to have a chance to talk to you!"

*Slap.*

The man covered his face and bowed his body.

"Just leave me be! Leave me alone!" The woman shouted.

*It wouldn't be good if things went too far.* He hesitated, then stepped forward briskly.

"Anything wrong?" He asked.

The man froze under the streetlight like a wax figure.

The woman grumbled. "What took you so *bloody* long!?" She moved closer. "Just a drunk arsehole; let's go." She took his arm without glancing back.

He turned and looked. The man rested against a light pole, undoing his tie, his chest panting heavily like a dog.

Only after reaching Farringdon Road did the girl withdraw her arm. "Thanks, for now." She took out a cigarette from a leather case in her down jacket and lit it with a disposable lighter. "Would you like a ciggy? Silk Cut."

"No, I don't smoke."

"Even better," she laughed as she blew a smoke ring. "You know, there're plenty of kids in Madrid who started smoking at twelve or thirteen. I didn't start until I was sixteen; Quite an achievement, isn't it? I also started uni at sixteen." She eyed him. "Why didn't you stay with Kruz?"

"You know him?"

"Yes, a classmate of mine is his friend's girlfriend. It's complicated. Say we have mutual acquaintances."

"I see."

"You study Computing, right? At Imperial?" she confirmed. "Next time my laptop's giving me a headache, I'll know who to ask. But why didn't you stay with Kruz? Summoned away by your sweetheart?"

He laughed. "Not really. But I was summoned, alright." He paused. "My name's Chance, and as I was passing down the road, I heard someone needing a chance."

"A chance. I wish I had a chance...or a choice, even." She ruffled her hair with one hand. "You know what people say? That talk is cheap." She smoked as she pondered. "Thanks anyway. Sorry that I couldn't buy you a drink. Perhaps I'll make it up to you sometime. We do have quite a reading list for the reading week." She stomped her knee-high boots and stopped a cab. "Let's see when fate shall let us meet again. Farewell, comrade!"

Fate certainly had more in store for the two.

*Two weeks later.*

As he headed towards the building exit, he heard someone call him from behind.

He turned back and saw Isabel stepping out of the lift. She had a black Brompton folding bike in one hand and a silver cycling helmet in the other.

"Hey! What brought you here?" she walked up and asked.

"Well..." He looked out of the window. "The east wind, maybe."

"Ah, the notorious east wind!" Isabel exclaimed. "The Great Fire of London would not have started if not for that." She eyed him suspiciously. "Seriously, are you here to stalk me?"

"Believe it or not, I'm here for a class."

"At this late hour?" She checked the clock on the wall behind her. It was well past nine in the evening.

"Not a university course; an evening language class. For Spanish."

Isabel put down her bike and elbowed him. "I didn't know you spoke Spanish!"

"My stepmother is Mexican, and she wanted me to learn. I've missed the registration at Imperial, so I ended up here."

"*Qué mona!* My mother's a Spanish teacher for foreign learners." Her eyes brightened with excitement. "You know what she has always said about improving language skills? The best way is to practise with a native speaker. We can talk in Spanish from now on! Or you know what's better? Why don't you also ask your stepmother to learn Chinese? You can race her."

They walked out of the building as they talked.

"She's half-Chinese," he explained.

A few students idled by the one-metre-high stone platform outside the gate, smoking.

"Can I borrow a light?" Isabel took out a cigarette and asked someone nearby. The other party agreed. "Do you have any plans for tomorrow? I've got a *fiesta* at my place, and I promise you'll meet a lot of native speakers."

"Sorry. I have a school project tomorrow."

"What's it about?"

"Software that helps people with hearing loss. We're trying to set up a translation service between British Sign Language and spoken English."

"Sign language, you say?" Isabel puffed as she smoked. "I know someone who learnt sign language for his DofE."

"Guess what this means in British Sign Language." He held up his left hand, made a gesture of 'one', then made circles around his left ear several times.

She thought carefully. "To slow down?"

"Well…" He could not resist showing off. "This sign means 'London'. It's said to indicate the chimes of Big Ben." He looked at the bus schedule and took out his jingling coin case. "My bus's here. Hope you have a good night."

"Last time I owed you a beer, and this time you owe me a party. We'll settle our bill next time!"

A week later, he met her again after his Spanish evening class. This time, she did not have her bike but carried a tote bag with her law school logo.

"How was your class?" she joked as she approached. "When are we switching to Spanish-only conversations?"

"Perhaps we should wait for another decade or so."

"And how is the software going? Well?" She said as she made the sign for London.

"Not bad."

"Care for a drink now?"

He thought for a while. "Sure, why not."

They ended up at The Seven Stars on Carey Street. He had never been to that pub. Some legal professionals wore wigs while they drank and laughed.

"Why don't you tell me more about yourself?" Isabel asked as they found a corner seat. "For starters, why did you choose to study in London?"

He responded as he nurtured a beer. "Well, long story short, I loved Sherlock Holmes as a kid. And Australia seems too far, Canada too cold, I had already been in China, the US, and Japan, so the UK was one of the few options left."

Isabel emptied her glass. "And do you find London up to your expectations?"

"Not bad. Except for the rain, which makes Australia a little more attractive," he laughed. "Someone on my course made a bet and vowed never to use umbrellas throughout the four years. Many of my classmates think he won't make it. But he made it so far."

"My cousin lives in Granada, and she loves the London rain. Where she lives, it's sunny all year round; you wouldn't even see a cloud in a month. Well, maybe that's exaggerated…There's a Spanish word for the kind of rain in London: *sirimiri*. You should check it out. It's a super cool word."

He smiled. "If I learn one new word every day, I could master the language in no time."

"And have you been to the Sherlock Holmes Museum?"

"Hmm…" He raised his beer, but his hand stopped in mid-air. "To be honest, I was disappointed…especially when you step out, and you see a Tube station and people queuing; it's not quite the scene in the book. Baker Street is too modern now."

"Did you know that Baker Street Station is one of the world's earliest Underground stations? I have a friend who works there. The Museum. Volunteering. And to become a volunteer, you need to show your enthusiasm and passion for the story."

He nodded. "Now that you know why I'm in London, why you are here?"

"Well, that's simple enough. My papa is a lawyer, and he wants me to become one as well. Law is something where you need both hard work and connections to have a successful career. We just had a departmental event, and I was able to invite a barrister. An OBE. His name is C – Look!"

Chance's eyes followed her finger. In the opposite corner, a black cat was licking its front paw.

"That's Thomas." She waved at the cat, but he ignored her. "I love cats." Isabel turned back. "I have two super cute Siamese cats and two super annoying sisters at home in Madrid."

"I have a cat as well. Sonic. After Sonic the Hedgehog."

"You have no siblings?"

"No."

"Oh." The answer dawned on Isabel. "One-child policy, isn't it?"

"Yes."

"Quite a few families in Spain have adopted Chinese girls. My mom has a friend who married a Chinese man, and they had a boy. One day, her friend was shopping with her baby son, and someone stopped them to ask how she had managed to adopt a boy."

As she recounted, her speech halted, and her gaze shifted…

\* \* \*

"Now, I'm really worried that this place is haunted," Felipe watched his temporary roommate. "Your mind seems to be roaming around. Yet, your body is like a tin man. Eh, *estás en Babia!*"

Chance gathered himself.

After parting with Tilly, memories had flooded over him.

Felipe dragged a chair across the floor and sat down, crossing his legs. "You have fifteen minutes. You do know the fifteen-minute rule, don't you? That presidents only have fifteen minutes to listen to their ministers to make significant decisions. Be sincere, be brief, be seated. In other words, make it snappy. So, you now have my precious fifteen minutes."

"For what?"

"Anything. We can discuss anything." Felipe thought for a while. "If Tilly Wurman had used Joyce Peng's spare key to get into her room, do you suppose that on the night of the fire, Joyce Peng also used Tilly Wurman's spare key to let herself into her house? Before Tilly came back from work, that is."

"It could be."

Felipe sucked his gums. "Or it could be easier than that. A peek through her mailbox might be informative enough."

"Could be."

"Define 'disappointment'. It's twelve, and you are as hungry as a puma and would like some ickenchay oupsay. But the lady in the takeaway says it's not time for lunch yet."

"Umm…"

"You know, I've always found you to be on the quiet side. But recently, you seem to be sulking. A lot."

"Perhaps."

"Here, it goes again. One-word answers."

"If you say so."

"Ah. That's better."

Felipe smiled mysteriously. "Cecil Stone called me earlier. It seems that Catherine has changed her mind, after all. He would cover for her time at work. Her uncle could cover her during the evenings. So, you need to fill in the gaps. He wants you to meet her in front of One Aldwych tomorrow morning at ten."

He was in no mood to reply.

"And I'm taking the Rover to golf in the morning, so you'll have to take a cab or the Underground."

"Bus will do."

He reached for his jacket and took out his coin case, the same one he'd been using six years ago. There were not many pound coins in it.

Felipe yawned. "I have a theory about why people like to read on the Tube, or the Underground, or the Metro, or whatever they call it here in London. Isn't it because the signal reception is too bad that they have no other choice?" Then he stood up and vanished into the bedroom.

\* \* \*

14th April.

"Missy, do you want to take the Big Bus Tour?"

Catherine was standing in front of One Aldwych as a man in sunglasses approached her.

"No, thank you." She took a few steps back, clutching her bag.

*Why do sunglasses still function with a missing lens,* she reflected as she waited.

Everything had looked fine on her way to work yesterday morning.

*What physics could explain that?*

She blamed herself for making such a fool of herself.

Catherine looked at her watch. Five past ten.

The man hadn't shown up yet.

*He wasn't rude, but he was late...*

She had been fervently against the whole 'bodyguard' idea. But when she got back home yesterday, she had seen the man who broke her kitchen window across the street.

He looked at her. A bus passed. Then he was gone.

*Vanished into thin air...*

Catherine had reeled on her way back. And Mrs Ferguson's visit did not help at all. Her neighbour had witnessed a suspicious figure looming in her back garden on several occasions: a huge man in a green trench coat with a scar on his face.

She called her uncle, then Cecil. They agreed that she could leave her job at the Chamber on one condition: that she would allow some assistance.

And now, as Catherine waited in the biting wind, she felt silly and annoyed.

She turned back.

Cecil was meeting a client at the hotel lobby. He saw her through the

SHAWE RUCKUS

window and nodded as if telling her to be patient.

Catherine waited and tied back her hair.

The tour bus arrived. Its doors opened, and a group of tourists eagerly hopped down.

"Sorry to keep you waiting, Miss Roxborough." The same man who had advised her on her eyewear yesterday came down from the bus and stood in front of her.

"No, not at all. I…I hope you had a good sightseeing session. First time in London, huh? I sincerely hope the scenery was good enough to delay you for more than a quarter of an hour."

"I'm truly sorry. I just found out that it is no longer possible to travel on the bus without an Oyster or a contactless card. So, I took the tour bus," he explained.

*Time could change many things. The law school at King's College London had a new name, and London buses no longer accept cash.*

"I'm sorry for being late," he apologised again. "I see that you managed to reconfigure your sunglasses."

"Yes."

Catherine had found the missing lens under her sofa at home yesterday afternoon.

"I'm not sure how you're going to assist me exactly." Catherine tilted her chin up. "I'm not going to have a CCTV system installed in my house. If you want to follow me around, that's fine. Don't tell me where to go or what to do. I'm more than capable of taking care of myself. So just let me be, really."

The man lowered his eyelids and finally raised his head. "Of course. Miss Roxborough, if you wish me out of your sight, that can be arranged."

* * *

*Later.*

Chance had followed her to a furniture store, a bookstore with an extensive collection of maps, then to a second-hand clothing shop called Rokit.

After seeing her back to Cecil Stone's office, he grabbed a quick lunch at a sushi chain and then headed to Joyce Peng's apartment.

He called the lift and waited, but it seemed to be stuck on the ninth floor.

He waited a bit longer and finally decided to take the stairs.

When he arrived upstairs, he found an elderly Caucasian woman in the lift, busy schlepping family-sized packs of toilet paper.

"Oh, sorry!" she exclaimed. "You must need the elevator. Give me a sec." She had a Virginian accent. She did not wait for his reply but continued. "Had a big discount on Ocado. It could never hurt to stock some of 'em like my grandma used to say." She patted the unopened boxes of toilet tissues and smiled. "Who doesn't like to save a few bucks?" "Howdy!" She reached out her hand eagerly, "Hannah Robinson. My husband and I are staying at number four."

They shook hands, and Chance introduced himself as someone who had come to inspect apartment five.

"That bad with number five, huh?" She lowered her voice. "We never had the chance to meet her. Perhaps it was a good thing that we didn't know her, or it would've been worse."

He didn't say anything but directed his attention to her boxes. "Perhaps I can give you a hand."

"That'd be great!" She thanked him as she handed him three packets of toilet tissue.

They passed the atrium and found their way to apartment number four.

"Sarnai? Darling, would you mind helping us get the rest of the toilet rolls?" She pulled her front door open and shouted. "They're in the elevator!"

A younger woman in an apron appeared from the kitchen and quickened her steps. She had high cheekbones and a round face. "Yes, Mrs Robinson. Are you keeping them in the bathroom upstairs?"

"We'll see. I'm afraid there ain't enough space. The water company said they still need to check the pipes."

Chance put down the packs in a corner and asked, "Were you away during the fire?"

"Oh, yes. We're glad that we were." Hannah Robinson roamed around the living room and put down her portion of toilet tissues. "Eddy and I went on a hiking trip to Austria. We only got back last week." She thought for a while. "It's such a shock to our poor Sarnai. She even told us that she was planning to go back to Mongolia, but we've managed to persuade her to stay." Then she added, "Must be hard, for your business as well. Houses, where people died, are hard to lend."

She seemed to have mistaken him as someone from NP Properties.

"Yes," he said, "especially in this case."

Sarnai struggled with five packs of toilet tissues; she almost lost her balance entering the narrow door. He noticed that she had written something on the back of her right hand. A few rolls of paper escaped their packaging and dropped on the floor. He bent down and retrieved them. "You were there…that day, in apartment five, right?"

"Yes. And I am going to get a divorce." The cleaner pursed her lips. "I'm staying here for my daughter. If I had a choice, I would not stay. Not after what I saw."

Hannah Robinson offered him a glass of iced tea. They talked about the plants that she had grown in the atrium. Then he returned to apartment five.

He ventured upstairs into the study and sat down in front of the desk.

He tapped on the keyboard. Still no response. He checked the power cord; all seemed fine.

He thought for a while and pressed the brightness button several times. The screen finally lit up.

It didn't take him long to jack into the system. A dog's smiling face greeted him. He checked Joyce Peng's email: two new messages. One was from the Maughan Library requesting an unreturned book. The other was spam. Her browsing history showed an almost impressively long list of websites on various suicide methods.

He recovered the deleted files up to three months ago. A quick look through did not tell him much.

He shut the device down and rummaged through Joyce Peng's desk drawers. There was a library card issued by King's College London.

He pocketed the card and picked up the book to be returned, the one on suicide.

Then he took the lift downstairs and found his way to the Maughan Library.

A white BMW was parked not far from the entrance. A Deliveroo rider was anxiously contacting her customer.

He took out Joyce Peng's library card, the photo side to his palm, and beeped in. The security paid him no attention.

There was a place for self-returning and borrowing. He watched as a machine processed the book.

He beeped himself out. A few students were smoking and discussing their term papers on the stone steps. Someone explained why the library had been in lockdown during the Holborn fire.

A statue of Confucius stood not far off on freshly cut grass.

He remembered visiting Isabel once in this library. She had told him of the secret apartment that the library kept for the College Principal and rumoured rooms to be haunted. She introduced a friend to him, a varsity tennis player she had met in a mooting competition. She looked both beat and high that time. He wondered if she had been using the drugs since then.

His phone rang as soon as he exited the library.

Felipe directed him to a steakhouse called The Gaucho on the same lane.

When he entered the restaurant, he found Felipe seated at a window table. There were mineral water and a basket of cornbread on it.

"One good thing about being an adult is, you can decide what to eat, where to eat, and whenever you wish to eat," Felipe said as he sat down. "I'd say that's freedom. And not so many can afford this type of freedom. There are set times to go to work, set times to leave work, set times for lunch breaks, and set times for tea breaks. I only have three things that I look for in a job: that I can eat whenever I want, that I can go to the loo whenever I want, and that it has good pay." He arranged the cutlery and made room for his entrée.

Felipe continued. "Ever heard the phrase that you are your own greatest enemy? Complete bullshit. Your enemy is everyone but you! It's the guy who pushed you out of the company because his dad was someone important, or the one who wooed your girl because his family is richer. Our worst enemies are never ourselves; we are our own greatest allies. No one can change you easily except yourself." Felipe laughed. "I have no intention of patronising you; consider this a little side mentoring." He handed Chance the menu. "Ever wondered why Gauchos are often depicted in military uniforms with their *mate* in hand?"

"No."

"Well. Now you should be." Felipe leaned back. "The Turkish army had ordered a batch of uniforms from France during the Crimean War, but the battles ended soon after. Having no other places to sell them, a French diplomat managed to convince an ambassador to dump the uniforms on the Argentineans. A good case study of international trade, one might say."

Chance drank some water. "I was at Joyce Peng's apartment just now. I didn't find anything particularly useful."

"Let me quote my Marketing professor from Harvard Business School: data collected consists of facts and errors. Now tell me about Joyce Peng: was she contented or disappointed the moment before she died? You'll need at least three different data sources to confirm this. The ex is one, the music teacher counts as one, so who else might be there? You make me feel like we're in a two-hour exam, but you decided to submit your paper after ten minutes." He looked all serious, then suddenly laughed. "You should carry out this investigation like a forensic accountant. As Sam Antar said, talk to ex-lovers, ex-employees, and employers to rat out management. You might as well check if she had bought any lottery tickets. I'm happy to split the prize fifty-fifty."

Chance thought for a while. "I'm not sure if there is anything else that I can do."

"You haven't met Joyce Peng's tutor from university, have you?"

"No."

"Then that's where you'll go next."

A waiter approached and asked, "How do you find your meal, sir?"

"Don't call me 'sir' because it makes me feel old. But the food is not bad. At least the portions are a good size," Felipe remarked. "I hate small portions of everything, especially if the food is bad." He laughed. "James Bond said that."

"Very well…Please enjoy your meal."

"I've been re-reading the Bond series lately. My favourite was *On Her Majesty's Secret Service*. But really, if the agents never find their true love or always fail to protect their loved ones, do they dare to claim themselves to be the best?" Felipe wondered. "And this Fleming fellow really could use some fashion design tips. All he seems to know about traditional and cultural East Asian wear is kimono. I bet the majority of Western writers could not differentiate between *kimono* and *yukata*. I can hardly picture Dr No wearing a kimono. Do you know who else might benefit from East Asian Costume 101?" Felipe picked up his knife and cut through the grilled chicken breast. "When I was in high school, the only book in our library available in English was *Casino Royale*. I read it, and I thought, how cool would it be to cry tears of blood?" He looked up. "But I've learnt a lesson from Le Chiffre as well: don't touch anything that does not belong to you."

Felipe's phone vibrated, and he checked his message.

"Catherine is going to a flower market tomorrow afternoon. Her uncle will be teaching, so you'll need to fill in." Felipe put down his phone and gave Chance a meaningful glance. "I don't mind if you keep yourself out of her sight; just don't lose her out of your sight."

# CHAPTER 7

*I love Catherine.*
*I will not let anyone hurt her again.*

## 15th April

At one fifty p.m., he showed up in front of South Kensington Underground Station. The noticeboard at the entrance had all sorts of higgledy-piggledy ads: lost and found, missing pets, day-care, tenants seeking, and romantic rendezvous. He put away his black folding umbrella and read as he waited.

A boy was standing beside a pillar nearby. He munched on a sandwich, also waiting for someone. A few minutes later, the boy's friend arrived. They held hands and went into the station.

He picked up a free newspaper and leaned against the wall, filling in the crossword puzzle in his head.

Another five or so minutes passed before Catherine appeared. She got out of a Jaguar and waved at the driver. She wore a pair of red trousers, ankle boots, and a white blouse with prints of cartoon dinosaurs that day.

"Hello," she took off her sunglasses. "I thought you might be late today as well."

"I try not to make tardiness a habit." He tucked his newspaper back into the stand. "I'm familiar with this neighbourhood."

"Cecil told me that you went to Imperial. His daughter Sophie went there as well."

"Miss Roxborough, have…have you ever visited her there?"

"Yes, quite a few times." Catherine seemed a bit surprised by his question. "We better get going. Let me see…we can take the Central Line from here and head to Holborn. Were you able to get an Oyster card?"

"Yes, I managed to get one."

"Then let's set off." Catherine took out her card and headed towards the entrance.

"Miss Roxborough…" The man called behind her. "There…there is a…"

"Yes?"

"Would you just stay still for a moment?" he asked as he got out his phone and took a picture of her back.

*I wonder what he's playing at.*

The man was somewhat awkward when he showed her the photo.

A long white feather dangled right in the middle of her derrière. Her red trousers certainly did a good job of contrasting the whiteness.

*Lordy! Must be the quill cushion!*

Her hands hurriedly reached the seam of her trousers and removed the foreign object.

"Thank you, Mr…" Catherine handed him his phone.

"My last name is Yang."

"Yang as in 'Yin Yang'?"

"Not really. You can call me Chance. Chance would be fine." The man paused. "Would you like me to be out of your sight today?"

143

Catherine thought for a few seconds. "No, I don't think that'd be necessary."

They took the Central Line, changed at Holborn, and finally arrived at Bethnal Green Station.

A few elders were discussing the tube shelter disaster on their way out.

"Is the Columbia Road Flower Market only open on Sundays?" he asked as they made their way towards it.

"Not quite. I'm going to a crafts store that's only open today." Catherine smiled uneasily. "Thank you for coming along. Cecil and my uncle mollycoddle me at times. They seem to enjoy cossetting me. I know this is perhaps not the best time for me to be out alone."

"No worries at all." He noticed a pickpocket who was eyeing his bag. He adjusted his messenger bag's position. "I would appreciate it if you could tell me more about the...stalker. Are we sure that he *is* a stalker?"

"There's really not much to tell," Catherine sighed. "Last Monday, I came home. I had been abroad for a while. I was unpacking while talking to Cecil on the phone. Then I heard someone shouting outside my kitchen window. Cecil heard it too. There was a man with a *scar*, a long scar, on his face, standing outside my kitchen window. He was shouting wildly. And he smashed the window."

"I heard that the police were not very helpful."

"No, they were not," Catherine continued. "Then the other day, I saw him across the street, watching me. A bus passed, then he was gone. My neighbour told me that there was a man in a green trench coat in my garden, quite suspicious."

"Have you received any messages containing harassment or threats on your phone? Or in your mail? Or over Bluetooth?"

"No…not that I remember," Catherine recalled as she hurriedly turned off the Bluetooth function on her phone.

"And you haven't seen him around your office?"

"No."

"Are you safe during the evenings?"

"Yes." Catherine nodded. "I'm staying over at my uncle's place. He and his girlfriend. Her parents came to visit; I feel safer with people around me."

"Are Mr and Mrs Roxborough away?"

"Yes, they are away."

*Far away.*

She hesitated. "They passed away."

"I'm sorry." He thought. "Did you notice anything different in the house after you came home last Monday? Say, an extra piece of furniture you've never seen before, or an ornament that you didn't recognise? Some people take advantage of vacant houses when the owners are…away."

"I don't think so." Catherine tilted her head. "Cecil would sometimes come to the house to sort out the utilities."

"Well, if you see him again, and I'm not there, could you inform me asap? Don't confront him. If he tries to approach you, try to stay away from him as far as possible."

"I know better than to confront him. Probably I would if I were a Kung Fu master or a Special Agent." Catherine gave a small laugh. "I will run away…"

*I am very good at running away from my problems.*

"Here's my number." The man gave her his card. "I keep my phone on in the evenings."

Catherine took the card and stored his number as a new contact.

The card read:

Changxi Yang

M&A Consultant

Mercury Investments and Securities

*Not Yin Yang's Yang…*

She put away his card as they walked.

"Mr Yang, hmm…Have you ever done this before?"

"As in?"

"Anti-stalking…consultation."

"Not on the receiving end. I'm afraid."

"As in?"

"Miss Roxborough, we did track people down. Sometimes."

"I see."

"Now that you have decided to leave your job at the Chamber, would you still go to Mr Stone's office in the daytime?"

"Well. That's not entirely practical, is it?" Catherine mused. "I guess I should stay low until the whole issue resolves." They stopped at a roadside sweet shop. "Do you mind if we pop in really quickly?"

"Not at all."

"There's something that I was looking for."

Catherine pushed open the parquet wooden door.

"Who was the actor who played Albert, Duke of York, in *The King's Speech*?" In the corner of the shop sat an elderly lady in a wheelchair who had asked the question.

"Colin Firth." She froze for a moment, then quipped, "Is there a discount for the correct answer?"

"Please, I'm sorry for the trouble." A middle-aged man stood behind the cashier. "My mother's very fond of pub quizzes before she's taken ill."

Catherine looked around. "Do you happen to have any flying saucers?"

"Sorry, luv, they're out of stock. There's a bit of a conflict with the doctor's appointments. I haven't had time to stock up."

"It's fine," Catherine grabbed a pack of barley sugar. "I'll take these." She paid with her card.

The shop's door opened, and a couple walked in. The man wore a pink shirt with shorts and white loafers. He had no vest on, making his chest hair highly visible. The woman was slender and tall. She had a long skirt that almost floated as the door closed.

"Who was the actor who played Albert, Duke of York, in *The King's Speech*?" the lady in the wheelchair asked again.

"Darling, do you know?" The woman's face tightened. "I don't usually watch movies with heavy plots like that."

"I don't either…" The man fidgeted. "Probably…Hugh Grant? Say, mate, do you have any flying saucers here?"

Catherine looked up.

*No!*

*Why now? Why here?*

Her ex-fiancé noticed her as well.

"Cathy…" Pierre's eyes dodged hers. "When did you get back?" His hand snaked onto his companion's waist. "This is Patricia…I believe you've met her before."

Catherine recognised her as the daughter of the owner of a restaurant near Pierre's flat. They had matching diamond rings on their fingers. They shone too piercingly.

"Hi." Catherine reached out her hand. "Pierre's sister and I went to the same university." She turned to Pierre. "Yes, I'm back. It's good to be back."

"And this is?" Pierre looked at her and the man beside her.

"A friend," she stated simply.

"A friend?" Pierre's eyes questioned.

"Well, Catherine."

Her heart jumped a bit at the man calling her by her first name.

"We still need to go to that crafts store." He turned and spoke to Pierre, "So we won't delay your friend any further." He added, "It's a pity that the flying saucers are out of stock."

As they left the sweet shop, Catherine felt a little uneasy. "Have you ever heard the expression about a blind dog hunting deer?" she asked rhetorically. "No matter how hard you try, there are still things…" She trailed off.

They walked in silence for a while, not long before Catherine found the purpose of their visit.

The crafts store had various tools and kits for DIY home products. It also hosted a small jewellery section with glass cabinets taking up most of the back space. The shop assistant received them eagerly.

"Do you mind if I look at this pair of earrings?" Catherine asked as she browsed through the collection of accessories featuring animals made from ceramics.

"The bees? Oh, they're lovely. And they go well with your skin tone too." The shop assistant unlocked a cabinet as she presented the earrings. "And they're the only pair we've got; look, here's the mirror."

Catherine tried the earrings, and she liked them. "How much are they?"

"Forty, my dear, and we're cash only."

"Oh." A look of regret crossed her face, "Perhaps you could point me to the nearest cash machine? I'll be right back."

"It won't be a stroll in the park, I'm afraid." The shop assistant took the bee earrings back and locked them up again. "The closest one is broken. You have to take a right off the main road, and there's a Halifax two lanes away."

"Sweetie, aren't these cute? Little bees…"

A voice reminded Catherine that they were not the only customers in the store.

A teenage couple stood in front of the glass cabinet and gazed over the items.

"I'll buy them for your birthday, 'kay?" the boy offered.

"That's a big no-no," the girl giggled, "a birthday gift has to be a surprise. Why don't you buy them as a gift to celebrate my birthday one-month countdown?"

The boy grimaced.

"Or I could buy them for myself." The girl opened her bag. "We girls should be financially independent."

Chance listened as the pair interacted. Then he walked over to the cashier, drawing the shop assistant's attention. "We'll take them. Please wrap them up. And I'd like a receipt."

"Oh, I could hardly let you…" Catherine protested.

"It's fine, Miss Roxborough. Please do not be concerned." He smiled as he handed over two twenty-pound notes.

\* \* \*

"Do you like bees?" Isabel asked as he ate.

"I hate them." He put down his chopsticks. "When I was a kid, I was stung by wasps once. Took me weeks to recover."

"If you are in an interview and the interviewers ask you this question, you have to say you love bees. If they ask you, what is your favourite animal? Bees are the correct answer. They are hardworking. They have teamwork; they are loyal; they are productive…Bees are the answer."

"Not ants?"

"Well…ants might do, but they sound so unoriginal. You can't expect to make a good first impression." She laughed. "And after all the turrón and all the Pifarré honey sweets you've had, you should be grateful to bees for their hard work."

* * *

"Would you like some coffee?" a distant voice asked.

He gathered himself. Catherine was pointing to a café.

"No. I don't drink coffee."

"Some tea then?"

He took a deep breath. "Yes, tea sounds fine."

A waitress led them to the rooftop area and a two-seat table. They took their time with the beverage menu and ordered.

"I'll pay you back as soon as I find a cashpoint." Catherine held the little velvet jewellery box. "Thanks a lot."

"There's really no need. I get my expenses reimbursed anyway." He thought for a while. "And if no one spends, the economy will halt."

Their drinks came. Catherine had a peppermint tea, and he an Earl Grey. He steeped his tea bag for a while.

"Milk?" she asked as she lifted the pitcher.

"No, thank you." He looked around and found what he needed. He took the salt dispenser and added a little.

"Hey, that's not sugar!" Catherine spluttered. "It's salt!"

"Yes. I know." He put down the dispenser. "I like to have my tea with a little salt. It's a tradition in my hometown."

"And where is your hometown?"

"It's a small place in China." He paused. "You probably don't know it."

He sipped his tea. The salt tasted as salty as any tears can be.

\* \* \*

"Sal!" Isabel stood on the couch and shouted.

He ran into the kitchen and grabbed the salt dispenser. "Here you go."

"No! Not sal! You get the hell out of here! How dare you plot against me? A secret birthday party, huh? You should always consult experts like me when organising parties." She grabbed a pillow and fought him.

"Stop it! Or I will…" He smiled mischievously. "Don't blame me later for destroying all your cushions."

"If I win, maybe you can adopt a panda for me through the WWF."

They fought and laughed, surrounded by flying feathers.

No one noticed the salt dispenser shattering on the ground.

\* \* \*

It started to rain on their way back.

In the end, Catherine did find a cashpoint, and he accepted the money willingly.

They followed the crowd out of Waterloo Station and entered an

Underground tunnel; its walls were inscribed with lines from a poem.

Someone was busking; It was Janet Seidel's 'When Lights Are Low'.

"I hope," he said, "that you can find your flying saucers."

"Yes, well…there's a stall selling sweets in Covent Garden. I might try my luck there," she said as her eyes followed the words on the wall.

His phone rang. It was Felipe. "Sorry, I have to take this," he apologised and connected the call.

"Sure."

"Did you have a good field trip?" Felipe asked. "As G.K. Chesterton would say, an adventure is an inconvenience rightly considered."

Chance could almost see Felipe smiling.

"The Japanese use the word 'aventure' to describe a romantic rendezvous, not knowing that aventure actually means death by accident as an obsolete legal term. Have you ever wondered why?"

"The stalker didn't show." Chance turned back; Catherine was on her phone talking as well.

"Let's have a little patience. Who knows, he might be lurking around the corner. Do you know what happens if a vegetarian cat meets a mouse? It says to the mouse; you are lucky that I don't eat meat; you are unlucky that my cousin does. Anyway, I'm calling to inform you that I'm on the Eurostar with Sara. You remember her, don't you? Sara White. The lady who thought you were my *boyfriend* (someone giggled uncontrollably in the background). She's nice arm candy. We're heading to the Hexagon for some spring shopping. The biddy lady upstairs has given me a lot of grief lately. I won't be back tonight, nor in a fortnight, and I've asked Johnson to deliver your luggage to Cecil Stone's office. I read an article earlier that the chances of Japanese and Korean cars being stolen are very slim in Spain.

Do you know why? It's not because they have better security systems, only because the gangsters cannot use the stolen parts incompatible with their cars. We may buy East Asian automobiles but never make ourselves useless. Value creation is difficult and…brutal. Catherine's family house is big and beautiful. You can make yourself useful there. And I'd say it's about time that you end your *sexenio**, and I find my *petite mort*."

"What about you?"

"*Amigo mío*, catching the mice was never a dog's job. My job is to oversee that you do your job. Remember to bring that taser with you."

The call disconnected.

He sighed.

\* \* \*

*A few hours later.*

He carried his suitcase into the hallway of Catherine's house.

"The cloakroom is this way." Catherine pointed to a wooden door on her right. "And the drawing room is in here." She gestured. "There's a guest room upstairs. I can go and prepare it."

"No. That will not be necessary." He followed her into the living room. "A couch will do."

He wondered how Joyce Peng felt when she stayed at Tilly Wurman's house.

A large rug welcomed them. The sofa had piles of cushions with different embroidered designs: cats, rabbits, chicken, and geese. A low bookshelf stood next to an LED TV. He stole a glance. Ian McEwan, John Banville, Sam Selvon, Monica Ali, Neil Gaiman, Kazuo Ishiguro, Paulo Coelho,

Mario Benedetti, Yu Hua, Alan Paton, Andrew Marvell, and a few books so old that their spines were hard to read.

The DVD storage had the *Twilight* collection, *Bridget Jones's Diary*, *Pride and Prejudice*, *Lark Rise to Candleford*, *Keeping Up Appearances*, *Line of Duty*, and some movies featuring Simon Pegg and Harrison Ford.

A carved wooden figure and a photo frame of Catherine with a group of children stood on the TV.

"Are you sure? This old treasure is no longer that comfortable."

"Statistics have shown that ground-floor and kitchen areas are most likely to attract unwanted guests as easy targets." He put down his suitcase and started to unpack. Then he saw Catherine striking a match and lighting a folded sheet of *Carta d'Armenia*.

The smell of vanilla spread.

He sniffed and sneezed.

"Bless you." She spoke. "Mr Yang, if you wish to smoke, please use the garden."

"I don't smoke."

"Oh...I thought."

"Felipe does. I guess I might need to find a better air freshener."

"Mr Yang, you only work with Felipe, right?"

"Yes."

She wanted to ask why they didn't stay at a hotel but decided against it.

"Are you certain you don't want a CCTV system installed? Or any tripwires around the house?" he asked.

"No!" Catherine exclaimed and laughed. "My life is not *Mission Impossible* or...a James Bond film. I don't know...perhaps a dog might help. But Mr Darcy will for sure put up a fight."

"For now, I'll install some motion detectors and a smart doorbell. For that, I need your WiFi password. Would you show me the kitchen as well?"

"Sure. The password is written on the wireless…thing. And follow me."

He took off his jacket and followed her through the dining room.

Felipe was right. It was indeed a large house.

There were pots of thyme and sage growing on the windowsill. The moon waxed outside in the garden.

A calendar hung on the refrigerator. It was for 2014.

The date 25th April was highlighted with the word 'Birthday' written beside it. There were some cooking books arranged on the top of the refrigerator.

The newly replaced window glass looked shinier than the stainless-steel tap. A big, ginger cat approached him cautiously.

"This is Mr Darcy." Catherine bent down and introduced them. "And this is Mr Yang. And no, his last name is not Yin Yang's Yang, and he prefers to have his tea with a little salt."

He laughed slightly. "My last name means 'poplar', as in poplar tree." He reached down to pet the cat. "Did Mr Darcy travel with you as well?"

"No. A friend was kind enough to take him in."

The cat rubbed affectionately against his trouser leg.

"He seems quite fond of you," Catherine looked up. "Please remember to shut the back door, or he might venture out. Mr Darcy is smart, like an old horse, and he knows his way around. But…still…we haven't been back for long." She picked up the cat and kissed him on the back.

He moved closer and tried to pet the cat again, but Mr Darcy caught his finger and bit him hard.

"Oh, I'm so sorry. Let me get you a plaster." Catherine pulled a drawer open. "I'm so sorry…he rarely bites. Now, Mr Darcy, you have behaved very badly!"

"I shouldn't have got that close." He turned on the tap and rinsed his wound. "I'm just a stranger in the house. He was right to have his guard up. I'll be careful with my fingers around him next time…"

He trailed off.

"Mr Yang?" Catherine asked. "Are you alright?"

The man sighed. "Yes. I'm fine. I just remembered that I need to check something."

He wiped his hand with some tissue Catherine gave him and put a plaster on his finger.

Dinner was simple: a salad with sautéed peas, tomatoes, avocado, and brown rice.

Catherine looked at the two sets of cutleries on the table, feeling a little lost.

*When was the last time this table hosted a dinner for two?*

"I'm a vegetarian…by my own standards," she said once they were seated.

He did not ask her to elaborate. He took up his fork and ate quietly. His injured finger did not give him much trouble.

Dessert was frozen pear with cinnamon, which he declined.

After washing up, Catherine sat down on a lounge chair in the living room with a cup of coffee.

*How exciting to do some job hunting*, she thought as she opened her laptop.

He checked the doors, locks, and windows. He also checked Catherine's network and made sure that no one had tampered with the settings.

The motion detectors were up and running.

He came back to the living room. Mr Darcy watched him from afar.

His eyes went over the bookshelf once more.

Sometime later, Catherine shut her laptop, stood, and stretched. "I think I might call it a night. There is a guest washroom down the hallway."

"Thank you, Miss Roxborough." He paused. "Do you mind if I ask you a question?"

"Fire away."

*We seem to be using the word 'away' a lot today,* she thought as she smiled.

"Have you read all these books?" The man gestured towards her bookshelf.

"Oh, yes. And some of them are quite well thumbed."

"Can you tell me how you felt when you read this one?" He pointed to a book by Paulo Coelho.

Catherine thought for a while. "Despite what its name might suggest, it's about death as much as it's about life and how we live life. You are welcome to read it if you want to."

The man nodded. "Thank you...and have a good night."

Mr Darcy reluctantly followed her upstairs.

* * *

*The next day.*

He opened his eyes at precisely five-thirty. He did not have a case of insomnia, nor did he wake up naturally.

He had had a dream.

*No chance to say goodbye.*

Then he struggled to breathe, only to find Mr Darcy the cat nestled comfortably on his chest instead of the sofa's arm.

"Can we make some peace?" he asked the ginger cat as he writhed below its weight.

Mr Darcy moved his whiskers but did not budge.

He craned his neck; Mr Darcy was as relaxed as a reclining Buddha. He remembered his injured finger before exchanging more morning pleasantries with the cat.

"If you let me do my job, how about I buy you three cans of your favourite cat food?"

The cat seemed to understand him and moved off.

He lay down again, trying to get some more shut-eye. Just as he was about to fall back to sleep, he felt something hot and wet flowing down his neck.

His first thought was that the ceiling had leaked. After all, it was an old house.

He touched his neck, then sniffed, and knew better.

It was eight o'clock when Catherine came down the stairs as she towelled her hair.

"Morning," she put down the towel and combed her hair.

Her guest was sitting by the dining table with his legs crossed, reading something on his tablet.

"I hope you slept well…" Catherine stopped as she found Mr Darcy balled up in a corner, cowering. "Oh! What have you done to my poor cat?"

"A more appropriate question, I believe–" he stood up– "is what has he done to me?"

"Did he try to bite you again?" Catherine eyed her cat and the man in front of her. "You said yourself that he could be anxious because of a stranger in the house. I'll use some cat calming spray."

"Yes, a stranger in the house." He pointed to a plastic bag on the floor. "I'm afraid that, from now on, I shall keep my belongings as far away from him as possible."

"Did he maul your shirt?"

"No, he did not maul my shirt," the man sighed. "He peed on me."

"What!?"

Catherine was livid and confused. Never in her time with Mr Darcy had she known him to pee on anything.

"Have you heard that cat's urine glows under ultraviolet light? I have a small tool here to help if you're interested in seeing this phenomenon." He held up a pen flashlight.

Catherine reached down and opened the plastic bag.

The shirt was a lost cause; no dry cleaner could save it.

* * *

*Two hours later.*

Carrying a small bunch of yellow roses, Catherine took out her keys and opened the door.

They had gone out for her weekly grocery, and she lingered at a florist's while her guest visited a nearby pharmacy.

Catherine unfolded her umbrella and put it in the stand by the door. Mr Darcy greeted her eagerly, meowing and swaying.

*Little devil.*

"You better treat our guest with more respect, Mr Darcy." She changed into her rabbit ear slippers as she reproached her cat.

He checked the locks, doors, and windows again.

Nothing was amiss.

By the time he got into the kitchen, Catherine was storing away her shopping in the fridge. She had also remembered to buy a new calendar for 2015.

"What would you like for lunch?" she asked as she replaced the calendar. The new one had a nature theme.

"I don't mind." He looked at the flowers, now neatly arranged in a vase. "Do you like gardening and floral arrangements, Miss Roxborough?"

"Yes, quite." Catherine put away her herb snips. "My parents loved gardening. They would visit the Chelsea Flower Show every year for days." She observed the tiny bubbles attached to the glass of the vase. "Wouldn't it be nice to spend your days surrounded by flowers and nice scents?" she looked at the comfrey and laurels in her garden.

"Perhaps you could consider a career in that field?"

She laughed and joked, "Yeah, perhaps you could write me a letter of recommendation?"

"I'm hardly in the position to do so."

"Nor do you have the authority," she recalled.

The man thought for a while. "Are you familiar with the meanings of flowers?"

"Well…I know the most popular ones."

"And…" He paused. "What might white roses mean?"

Catherine watched as rain rattled on her kitchen window. "Some send white roses to celebrate friends and family members' new beginnings. Weddings…Or to honour a friend…or to say goodbye, even. And roses are a safe choice. They are generally hypoallergenic…meaning that they are unlikely to cause pollen-related allergies. They are also safe for cats."

*This is not goodbye.*

He sat down on the sofa, lost in his thoughts.

"I think I might make some kale juice." Catherine sensed that it was perhaps best to end their talk.

The day passed uneventfully.

After dinner, Catherine curled up on her lounge chair, immersed in an Italian *Vogue* magazine. As she progressed through the pages, she couldn't help but notice the man sitting on the sofa, occasionally smiling in her direction. He had changed into a broadcloth shirt.

"Still thinking about your shirt, Mr Yang?" She put down the magazine.

"No." He put down his tablet, "Miss Roxborough, me being here, does it make you uncomfortable? Bother you, even?"

"I cannot say so," Catherine admitted. "But we did not meet for long."

"And not on such pleasant terms, if I may add." He smiled again. "Is there a trend nowadays to name your pets after book protagonists?" he smirked. "I was staying in a rented flat in Oval, and a neighbour had named her dog Mr Grey…" He paused. "I have to say that I'm rather good at noticing things."

"What are you getting at?" Catherine shot him a look.

"I have no right to comment on your reading options, in or out of your house. And I don't think that you need to hide or read discreetly in your own place. If you wish me to be out of your sight, that can be arranged."

"Perhaps you might be good at noticing things," she said, "but certainly not very good at keeping them to yourself."

Catherine closed the magazine on her lap and held up a copy of *Fifty Shades of Grey* high above her eyes.

\* \* \*

Mick called before she went to bed.

"Cathy, sorry for not being there, the party we had the other day with the troupe went all to pot. You sure you don't need me around? I could offer you a shoulder to lean on," he joked as she made her bed. "No, Micky, you better stay and stick with your wedding arrangements. I know it takes a lot of time and energy to prepare."

*From frigging first-hand experience as well.*

"My fiancé has helped me a lot. Thank heavens. He's in charge of the music. Did I tell you that he almost had a checklist in all the stores on Denmark Street? And how is Mr Darcy faring? I can say for certain that he does not miss us."

Catherine told him how her cat had bit and peed on their guest.

"No way!" Mick exclaimed. "Mr Darcy? He ain't a cute kitten, but he's a good cat. Why would he bite him? And why would he pee? Now I need to check if he contaminated any of our furniture. Did you say that cat's urine glows in the dark?"

"Some sorts of UV light."

She told him about her recent acquaintance and how they had met Pierre and his new love in the sweet shop.

"Salt in tea? Well, I've heard that in some places, people brew coffee with a pinch of salt in the water. Do you have any idea of the odds of running into a friend on London streets? It's about one in eight million, or so I've heard. Perhaps you should try your luck with EuroMillions."

"You know what, Mikey, I was worried about seeing him before I came back. I was gutted, really. Now I feel relieved, though. If he cheated once, he could do it again. It must leave her feeling insecure all the time."

"The daughter of that bistro owner in Islington, you say? The one we went to together?"

"Yes."

"Pierre is such an arse. Well, now we know that the fox may never grow good, but we surely have grown wiser. Perhaps you should come around next week; let's read our tea leaves. It's time to move on, Cathy. How could I enjoy domesticity when you are unaccompanied? Oh, I do hope that this tour ends well. It'll be my last choreography project as a bachelor."

They chatted for a while, and then Mick asked her tentatively. "Umm… Cathy, was Pierre…missing any fingers?"

Catherine winced, "No, not really. I don't think so."

Mick seemed relieved.

"But I did hear that he'd burnt his fingers in a Ponzi scheme. Cecil told me that his firm filed for insolvency. Guess it's just deserts."

After ending the call, Catherine locked her bedroom door so that Mr Darcy could not venture downstairs and do damage again.

*The next day.*

On their way back from the dry cleaner, Catherine spotted the man in the green trench coat.

He was following them, not too far away.

She tugged lightly on Chance's sleeve, drawing his attention. "He's here. Behind us."

Chance stepped aside, bent down, pretended to dust off his trouser' legs and peeked backwards.

The man was there.

"What should we do?" Catherine asked with unease.

"Keep going." He urged her to move.

A nearby shop window came in handy.

They watched as the man caught up with them.

Chance turned and saw the long scar on the man's face.

Then he stopped him.

# CHAPTER 8

## 18th April Saturday

Johnson called unsociably early in the morning.

"There's been a terrible accident here on the A4. Mr Kazama is waiting for you at the golf course."

Chance could hear incessant honking at the other end.

"It might be quicker if you go from there on your own. It won't take long from Oval."

It was all quiet in the corridor. The lady upstairs no longer needed to walk her dog.

He took the District Line and arrived at Kew Gardens Station almost an hour later. He found his way to Chiswick Bridge. There was a brown, brick factory across the river, with a giant Budweiser sign. A group of college students were rowing on the water.

He could hear aeroplanes taking off and preparing to land.

*Those out of the city want to come in; those in the city want an escape*\*.

He got off the bridge and followed an unpaved trail. It didn't take him long to find the golf course. He located the golf equipment store and found Felipe with the store staff, waxing about putter grips.

"Buddy! You've kept me waiting!" Felipe waved his hand at him. "You didn't dilly-dally, did you? Got any change on you? For the tokens."

He took out his coin case and paid for two driving-range tokens.

"Ah, Felipe! How are you today?" A short, middle-aged man walked into the shop. "Still after our early-bird discount, I see."

"An early bird gets the worm, but never be the early worm." Felipe flashed his smile.

Chance looked around. A leaflet on the bulletin board was not far from the door – a complimentary drink for players who arrived before eight in the morning.

"Coffee, tea, or beer?" a staff member asked.

"I'll have a beer. What about you, Raymond?"

"Nah," Raymond laughed, showing a crooked tooth. "My two boys are going to college in September. It's time to save up."

"Come on," Felipe said to Chance, "Ray will help you get some nice clubs. I'll meet you out there."

He followed Raymond and settled on some of his suggestions. Later, he stored his bag in a coin locker and went outside.

Felipe was sitting with a man he didn't recognise. They were talking and laughing over coffee. The man was well into his sixties. He had a polo shirt from Henry Cotton's and lacklustre hair mussed by the early morning breeze.

"Philip, I was wondering if you could lend me some of your grip on the Sovereign Gold Bond Scheme?"

"Sorry, Howard. Like many, I don't buy green bananas. Perhaps my buddy could help." Felipe gestured. "Allow me to introduce Howard McCain. Howard is a bigwig in the FMCG industry, and he serves on the board of an FTSE 100 company. They just completed an LBO. This is my assistant, Chance Yang."

They shook hands.

"Why, Ray, I see you've got a bit of a stiff left hand today, eh?" McCain observed.

"Don't mention it," Raymond laughed dryly. "Got hit by someone's ball on the course last week." He rolled up his shirt sleeve and revealed a burgeoning bruise. "Bad luck. That's all."

"Better than being hit with a club," Felipe cut in, "heard they hurt like hell."

"I've been coaching for years, and a club has never hit me." Raymond narrowed his eyes. "Do you gentlemen know the number one cause of death on the course? Heart attack. The business herd, sitting in their urban cubicles all day, come out and play in the sun. Tiring work."

"Which way would you prefer? Dying, I mean," Felipe asked. "In a small, locked room? Or out here in the fresh air? I don't want to go to heaven. None of my friends is there. And do you know what the original sin is? The US government debt. It's the seven-per-cent solution."

They laughed.

"You know, we do have a private joke among us trainers," Raymond continued; "a lady stated in her will that she wished to be buried on the course so that her husband would visit regularly."

There were only a few players that morning on the nine-hole course, and the ducks outnumbered them.

Howard McCain went to the parking area to fetch his glove, and Felipe warmed up on the driving range.

"Five little ducks went out one day~ Over the hill, and far away~ Mama duck said quack, quack, quack, quack~ But only four little ducks came back… Where did the straggler go? Camping, maybe?" he sang as he practised his tee shots.

Raymond gave a toothy grin. "Ducklings aren't bad. When I went for training in Florida, we had alligators roaming the course." He picked up his club bag. "I'll check the green first. See you in a bit."

"Okay!" Felipe responded happily. He waited until Raymond had walked out of their earshot.

"So," he turned to Chance, "no stalker after all?"

"No." Chance adjusted the strap on his cap. "Only a little misunderstanding."

"You know what people say about the mute and the dead? That they cannot speak for themselves." Felipe placed another ball on the tee. "Now the case is closed. No one is hurt. Just as you like it. Johnson told me an allegory once. It's called The Hunter and the Seven Swans. One day, a hunter sees a pack of seven swans and shoots one. The other six fled, and he took the injured back home. He wanted to kill it but decided to take pity on it. And the swan turned into a girl magically, and then he began to have some…evil intentions. In the night, the other six swans returned and together, they killed the hunter. The moral of this story is to be very careful with whom you bring home. And mercy for the enemy is an emergency for oneself."

"I should have noticed it earlier. I saw the missing pet ad he had placed the other day in front of South Kensington Station," Chance recalled. "The owner was looking for a ginger cat, male, neutered."

"Told you it would serve you well if you paid more attention to things." Felipe drove his club hard. "Have you heard the story of the old lady and the genie? One day, a genie appeared in front of an old lady and granted her three wishes. She said, 'make me rich'. And the genie did as he was told. Her chain turned into gold. Then she said, 'make me young again'. And the genie did as he was told. She was again a beautiful maiden. Then she said, 'turn my cat into a young, handsome prince'. And the genie did as told. Then the prince said to the old-lady-now-young-woman, 'now, aren't you sorry you had me fixed?'" Felipe laughed at this joke. "I'm not against anyone finding their pets, but don't you think they should do it without disturbing others? At least without breaking honest and peaceful citizens' kitchen windows?"

"He explained that he had meant no harm." Chance gazed at the artificial lake near the ninth hole.

"Oh, but good boys don't evade the police."

"He wrote to us that one time. He went to a pub, it was dark, and he was drunk. As he entered the pub, he didn't see the glass door and walked right into it, breaking his nose, leaving a scar. But the worst thing was that the pub owner thought he was there for trouble. They called the police; he couldn't explain himself; they threatened him. He hated it. He saw Catherine on her phone, and he thought she was calling the police, then he ran away."

"What about the time she saw him across the street, and he suddenly vanished?"

Chance smiled. "That was easy. He got onto the bus."

"All is well then. Guess we could only blame the poor quality of that window glass. Now Cecil Stone owes me a favour." Felipe put down his club and wiped his forehead with a towel. "I didn't know that you know British Sign Language. You certainly have more tricks in store than I'm aware."

"There was a project that I worked on in university."

"Well…old tricks never fail." Felipe smiled as his fingers played with the magnetic golf ball marker on his glove. "Before we start, today's game is not about winning. It's about losing. Losing elegantly and gracefully. This is not the time to play chicken but to play strategic idiots." He picked up his golf club bag. "Let's all aim for a triple bogey. Fake it till we make it. "

"How was Paris? You came back earlier than I expected."

"Young man, courting was never hard for me; the difficulties lie in the maintenance." Felipe gave him a sour face. "Yesterday, Sara and I had a row." He sighed. "It happened like this. I wanted a snack, so I took out a KitKat. She saw it and told me, 'Don't you know how many babies have died because of Nestle's inappropriate advertising? Its CEO even said that water should be privatised'. I said okay; so, I found a Snickers in my bag, and she told me that Mars supports animal testing. Then I asked, what about Cadbury's? She said that none of their cocoa beans was fairly traded. I have to say, her sense of justice has deeply marred my affection. I was thoroughly annoyed. I told her that whether it was fair trade or not, I didn't want to delegate my snack choices to some moral high ground. And now I'm getting the silent treatment."

Howard McCain waved at them on the course. They moved together downstairs.

"By the way, Johnson told me that he is willing to take us to some games for the July cricket season. We can go and have fun." Felipe laughed. "I would love to see this exotic sport in motion."

"July? Are we staying until then?"

Felipe took out a thermos from his golf bag, "Have you ever heard of a marketing term called 'genericide'? No, not genocide. It describes the process when customers think the trademark is the product's name, and the trademark loses its distinctiveness. Like Thermos…Brylcreem…Band-Aids. Even the word 'escalator' was a trademark once. Let's never lose our competitive edge. Remember, under promise, overdeliver. If we are to be spongers, at least let us leave a neat trail. When we finish our business, we can always revisit."

A caddie ran up and asked, "Mr Kazama, would you mind giving this sign-up sheet to Mr McCain? He forgot to sign it. I will come and collect it later."

"Let's not trouble you again." Felipe took out his fountain pen and signed. "See, as good as the original."

"Thank you, sir." The caddie left.

"I've heard the British summer is lovely. It would be such a shame to miss it. Look at us," Felipe mused. "We are in perfect sync with the three-six-three rule, borrow at three per cent, lend out at six, and have the day off every day at three in the afternoon. The world is bananas, but a Chiquita banana ends up very differently than an average banana." He looked away as Howard McCain walked further onto the course. "What a worry-free life we have."

* * *

*Eight hours later.*

"Oh, my back hurts," Felipe complained as they made their way back to their flat upstairs. "You better help me."

A neighbour went out with a bag of garbage and eyed them suspiciously.

"I'd love to use your device now," Felipe grinned and said to Chance loudly. "Your powerful device all over me, but I do hate getting sticky."

The neighbour escaped quickly, almost losing a slipper by the door.

"Doors are dangerous. They should be outlawed. Thankfully he didn't catch his neck in it*. As James Bond would say," Felipe laughed.

Back in their room, Chance sighed. "Your words could cause us trouble."

"See. Now you have first-hand knowledge of the constant discrimination that the LGBTQ+ community experiences daily. And it's okay if James

Bond says it and not okay if I'm saying it? Talk about double standards."

"A Chinese writer once wrote–" Chance charged his phone while he spoke– "that people's imagination runs so wild that as soon as they see short sleeves, they will think of bare arms, then nudity, then genitals, then the illegitimate child*."

"Pity that people don't need a licence to imagine, just as some don't need a licence to kill. And the illegitimate child is not a term that bodes well with the Catholic Church," Felipe ruminated. "Someone said that the Catholic Church and the mafia are two renowned organised bodies. But I say there is one fundamental difference. The mafia at least has the guts to admit their doings, while the other has no courage to admit their wrongdoings. Once I met a historian who had some interesting theories about the role Catholic priests played post-World War Two and how they helped Hitler to hide in Argentina. Fascinating episodes, I must say. Did you know that *Goldfinger* was once banned in Israel because the guy who played Goldfinger was a Nazi?" After a while, Felipe added, "Now, why don't you lend me your powerful device so I can recuperate some strength before dinner?"

Chance opened his suitcase and took out his electric muscle stimulator; the adhesive pads were no longer sticky and needed to be changed.

Felipe assembled the cords and pasted the pads on his calves. The tendons on his legs jumped as electric currents passed through them.

"This is so much better…" He closed his eyes.

Chance leaned against the door frame.

The cardboard box that he had used to trap the cockroach still stood where it was. He was not sure if the cockroach still lived or not.

Felipe must have sensed his unease, for he said: "A Russian idiom says that there are cockroaches in everyone's head, meaning that everyone is crazy in their own way. By the way, Mercury's business etiquette handbook requires us never to mention contract killing in the presence of Russian clients. And do you know that if you see a cockroach in your house, it means that there are probably a hundred of them unseen? Have you ever heard of a phrase called the 'dark figure of crime'? Just like crime: for every solved case, there are a hundred unsolved ones. Tell me, do you miss Catherine's clean, warm house?"

Chance ignored him.

He did miss Catherine's clean, warm house.

A house with a cat.

*No, not even the house.*

*Her.*

He wondered if she had remembered him.

He looked at his still plastered finger and smiled inwardly. He was sure that Mr Darcy had pulled tricks with him, perhaps out of jealousy. He still owed him three cans of his favourite cat food. He wondered if Catherine would let Mr Darcy eat vegetarian cat food. He wondered what she had meant when she said that she was a vegetarian by her own standards.

"If we're coming back in July," Felipe said with his eyes closed, "We better get some mosquito incense." He rubbed his temples. "I have a friend who lived in Madagascar as a child. He told me that people there used to put mosquito incense into empty beer bottles, and when the bottles were recycled, you could sometimes find the remains of burned incense in beers… a little *condiment extraordinaire*." He laughed, showing his gum. "It means that we'd need to stock some beer."

"I've heard that people who drink beer tend to attract mosquitos," Chance joked.

"Now you're just being wicked, aren't you?" Felipe opened his eyes and stared at him. "And Johnson told me earlier that Tilly Wurman is planning to quit her job. Did she tell you?"

"No."

"Her husband is being relocated to Shanghai, and she's going with him." Felipe moved the adhesive pads onto his arms as he looked at his shoes. "And did you know that there are two John Lobb companies? The first one is the old bootmaker on St. James Street in London; the other is a subsidiary that Hermès acquired. While the family workshop continues to operate in London, the part owned by Hermès has grown into a global chain of ready-to-wear shoes…" He sighed. "A man can never have too many pairs of John Lobbs. The authentic ones."

Chance reflected on his meeting with Tilly Wurman.

"The batteries just died." Felipe removed the adhesive pads and wrapped the cords into a coil. "Let's head out for dinner. I know a place that will not disappoint."

Dinner was at Mestizo, a Mexican restaurant not far from Euston. A banner inside said 'Spanish Only Please', and mariachi music played in the background.

"As a child, I never understood why psychopaths and serial murderers kill," Felipe scooped up a spoonful of *menudo** and brought it to his mouth. "If they loved the gore, send them to any slaughterhouses that supply pluck. Do you have any idea how much blood is shed when cleaning cows' stomachs and tongues? I promise you that they would never want to see blood again after a week." He gulped down his soup. "I don't know why I love *menudo* so much…perhaps it has something to do with Ricky Martin."

Felipe asked for another *menudo* as he reminisced about another of his part-time summer jobs.

Chance slowly ate his chicken tacos.

"Sara and I went to the zoo last week. They had guinea pigs on display. I told her that those will belong in the kitchen in Peru and that they are a national dish. She didn't believe me, and so I told her that, unlike Nestle's water source, Mother Nature's kitchen welcomes all. When she cried for my guinea pigs, I mourn for her turkey. Crocodile tears may be salty, but they do harbour problems. I've been more than pliant with her. I didn't even bring out the source of carmine in her red lipsticks." Felipe sucked his gum after hearing no response from his dinner companion. He said, "Come on, and now you are truly annoying; a Boolean data could do better than you. Not even a 'yes' or a 'no'."

Chance drank his lime-flavoured Jarritos. "Perhaps you could message her and ask her out. There are quite a few good Peruvian restaurants in London."

"And let her chide me over my snack options once more? She is no mouseburger, and I'm no longer a hayseed." Felipe shook his head. "That's hardly the dominant strategy. I don't wish to pop the clog on this relationship, not yet. Come to think about it, if life were indeed a box of chocolates, would you want it to be Snickers, or KitKats, or Dairy Milk bars? Perhaps Godiva sounds better. I'll make sure to search if the brand has any tainted past or failed marketing stunts before buying some. There are brands that, whenever you hear them, you wonder if your ears are playing tricks on you, like Arçelik, or Bimbo. But some other brands require second thoughts. Say, I would never go into a Scottish Widows branch unless I could meet one there…sounds like a good movie plot to me. And do you know what I'll do? I'll go to John Lobb's London store and have shoes handmade. Then I'm going to Stuart Phillips to get a new haircut. I heard it's the best hair salon in London." He smiled. "Johnson has made an appointment for tomorrow. In this case, even if she never texts me back, I'll still have a pair of new shoes and a new haircut. No use moping."

"Maybe more than a pair."

"Maybe. You know, you look sulky today. No, not today. Now," Felipe commented.

"I brought my stepmother here once."

"Ah, you rarely talk about her. Did she like it?"

"The food, yes. Not the name."

"Can't say I fancy the name either. Especially for us who have multiple… lineages." Felipe smiled. "I somehow feel that I would get along with your stepmother very well."

"Then I should be careful that you never meet her."

"Don't be so mean," Felipe loured. "Some people are born matchmakers. If you helped two single, middle-aged people find solace in each other's arms, how great a feat that would be!"

"Just wishful thinking on your part." Chance arched his brow. "She might be seeing someone now. We haven't talked for a while." He added, "Not since I came to London."

"Call it willful thinking. Where there's a will, there's a way. She's a jewellery designer, right?"

"Yes. For a niche brand."

"Did you hear about the Hatton Garden robbery?" Felipe mused. "What a great example of project management failure. They should do more preliminary research like watching *Flawless* maybe." He lifted his spoon and indulged in his second bowl of *menudo*. "Anyway, I look forward to being introduced."

After dinner, they took a cab back to Vauxhall Bridge and decided to stroll from there. Nothing seemed to have changed from the last time they had taken in the view from the bridge.

A small commotion caught their eye – a cyclist had been grazed by a car. Fortunately, there was no severe injury.

"During my university orientation, I remember a lecturer saying we should always wear a helmet while riding a bike in London. It would protect our brains, the most valuable assets we had. He also told us that it was probably the only time in our life that we can live in Kensington… because the house prices are so high there." Chance said as a car went by.

"Huh…Kensington – the very citadel of Victorian London."

"Lynette, my stepmother, always said that she was most proud of the fact that she had never received a ticket in the US." He paused. "But that doesn't mean that she never sped or anything. When the police looked at her driving licence, they took notice of her unblemished record, and they would let her go with a verbal warning."

"Ever did welding work? If the light is too strong, you get light blinding. If someone is too perfect, and if they shine too brightly…" Felipe searched for the miniature of St Paul's Cathedral. "Then we tend to overlook their small mistakes, which may grow like a dark hole. If murdering is a production line, will you be able to discover the bottlenecks on the *kanban* board?" He collected himself. "Enid called. The lady from NP Properties. She wants us to return the keys on Monday. I'll leave it to you. Oh, you can also visit Joyce Peng's university tutor on your way."

As they walked past the Oval, there was another abandoned beer can on the pavement.

"Durkheim defines suicide as any death, which is the direct or indirect result of a positive or negative act accomplished by the victim himself*,"

Felipe muttered. "If someone jumps the light and gets hit by a car, that's suicide. And all others who have invited dangers. It is a bit like *volenti non fit injuria*. Insurance only transfers the risk. Do you know what Sir Robert Anderson once said in his book, *Criminals and Crime*? He wrote, 'the humanity-mongers are so lavish of their pity for the criminals that they have none left for the victims; none for outraged society; none for honest and peaceful citizens impoverished by their crimes; none for the children they beget and rear to follow in their evil ways'. My old man died of liver cancer. There should be a line saying that smoking and drinking are harmful to your and others' health in every book."

"My dad died of lung cancer. He was a heavy smoker."

"In my view, in every book, there should be a drug dealer who is busted, someone who is punished for violating traffic rules, and someone who is caught when littering," Felipe walked up to the can and tried to kick it.

It was half full and soaked his John Lobb.

# CHAPTER 9

## 20th April Monday afternoon

The sky was cloudless.

Chance made the effort of walking from Oval to Covent Garden. It only took about an hour.

He inspected Joyce Peng's place again, and sometime later, he locked the door of apartment five as he heard someone behind him. He turned. Sarnai, the cleaner, was moving a large plant pot by Hannah Robinson's door. He offered help, and she accepted.

Some soil leaked from the bottom of the pot, and she went in for a dustpan.

"Is Mrs Robinson in?" He picked up some rotten leaves and put them in there.

"No. She volunteering at the Oxfam store." She paused. "If not, the gym."

He nodded. "Have they given you a key card for the lift when they are away?"

"Yes. I do their cleaning most of the time. When they travel, I water the tomatoes and the plants."

"I've heard the security system was down during the fire."

"Yes. So, the missus could come up."

She eyed the door of apartment five and remembered her first visit after the fire.

She remembered how much she wanted to forget and to undo time.

The man thought for a while. "Your name…Sarnai means 'rose', doesn't it?"

"Yes," Sarnai smiled. "Rose. My boss wants to list my name as Rose on our website, but I said no because that's not me. It's Sarnai."

She cleaned the area and dusted the doormat.

Chance told her that he had grown up in Inner Mongolia while she recalled a trip to Hohhot.

Ten minutes or so later, he bid her goodbye and went downstairs to return the keys to the front desk.

Sarnai also headed downstairs to receive a parcel from DHL delivered to the Robinsons.

She told him to have a good day again and followed him to the door.

The morning rain had made the marble floor slippery. Sarnai slipped and stepped on his right shoe, almost dragging a sock out.

He regained his balance, helped her stand, and reached out his hand.

She looked at him in mild surprise, smiled, and shook it.

\* \* \*

*Later.*

After three traffic lights, Chance found his way to the Strand Building.

He passed the single revolving door and walked down the connecting corridor on the ground floor to the King's Building.

The Easter holiday had just ended, and there were not many students on campus.

He checked the floor map and followed the stairs to the South West Block.

Some posters hung outside the bulletin boards of the Department of Music. One featured research on tuning a harp. He continued upstairs to the Department of Sociology. After a white door, there was a corridor with a warm green carpet and three offices. Alexander Roxborough's was at the far end.

He checked the time. He was early. A rattan basket sat on a table not far away, containing various mail addressed to the academic staff on this floor.

Tchaikovsky's music played in the office on his left-hand side.

He went up to Alexander Roxborough's office and knocked gently.

"Come in," a baritone voice said.

He turned the doorknob and went in.

"Oh! She loves tragedy and catharsis."

Alexander Roxborough was on the phone, and he gestured him to sit down.

"Last year, there was a production of *Electra* at the Old Vic. There were only two seats behind the pillars, but she insisted on us going. The stage effect was quite…Ha, ha. They built a real fire; someone choked on the smoke. That's the same footling complaint you make before every performance. I'm sure it will be alright at night, especially tonight. We'll see you later at the Palomar."

Chance sat in an armchair as his eyes took in the office setting.

It was of an unremarkable size, with university-standard bookcases, table, and computer. The Thames flowed behind the only window, and a set of Chinese shadow puppets decorated the wall on his right. The smell of freshly brewed coffee permeated the room. There was a box of chocolate pearls from Artisan du Chocolat on the shelf.

Alexander Roxborough continued to talk and laugh, his wrinkles stretching out. "Of course. You are most welcome to her exhibition. That's utter bilge! Oh, I'm sure we could accommodate you and Elise. Yes. I have a visitor now. Well, don't let those lager louts beat you, toodle-oo."

Alexander Roxborough put down the phone and stood up; Chance followed suit.

Chance introduced himself, and they shook hands.

"Cathy told me that you had been very helpful." Alexander Roxborough sat down and took a sip of his coffee. "We are so relieved to know that it was a misunderstanding."

Chance nodded. "I'm here today to discuss...to ask about Joyce Peng."

"Oh, Joyce. Such a poor thing," The professor furrowed his brows. "I remember she did her dissertation on the missing women in India...quite a nice piece of work."

"And she contacted you in mid-March, is that right?"

"Yes, well, she emailed, and I told her that we could meet over coffee after the Easter break."

Chance opened his bag and took out Joyce Peng's green diary. "There's a sentence she wrote that I don't quite understand." He read it out loud: "Even the LSE could not escape a manufactured risk."

Alexander Roxborough considered. "There is a British sociologist called Anthony Giddens. He was a Director of the LSE. He wrote a book called *The Runaway World*. He says that in the modern world, natural risks are becoming less frequent, but human-made risks are increasing. He calls them 'manufactured risks', like the Holborn fire, like production safety accidents."

"And Miss Peng didn't send you any other emails during the fire?"

"No."

"Thank you." Chance stood up. "I believe that's all."

Alexander Roxborough came from behind his desk and held the door for him.

"Mr Yang." The older man hesitated. "Perhaps you don't know me," he sighed, "but I know who you are."

By the time Chance got to Holborn Station, it was five-thirty.

He had remembered to buy a pack of batteries in a Boots.

"Thank you. Here's your change and receipt. Next customer, please," the cashier called.

He pocketed the batteries together with the receipt and ambled out.

Alexander Roxborough's last comment had left him bewildered. Had they known each other before? Had they ever met before? Not that he'd remembered.

Alexander Roxborough…Alexander…Roxborough…

The name did not ring any bells.

Who was Alexander Roxborough?

A sociology professor…Joyce Peng's personal tutor…and Catherine's uncle.

Who else could he be?

Someone tapped him on the shoulder, startling him. He turned around; a man of his age smiled at him. He was wearing a white shirt, jeans, and a pair of Fred Perry shoes.

"Chance Yang? I thought so." The man smiled. "Julian Lunn. You do remember me, don't you?"

*Ah.*

Julian, he did remember: a course mate from Imperial.

"Saw you with a girl the other day. If I didn't know any better, I'd say you were following her. Stalking her," Julian joked.

They chatted in a pub nearby.

He told Julian of his current situation, and Julian updated him on some of their friends. Nando, who dropped out of their course, now made his living as a paparazzo. Kruz had done another Master's at SOAS and gone back to Spain. Julian himself had worked for IBM and was now a systems engineer for a start-up in Cambridge.

They exchanged business cards not long before Julian received a call.

"Sorry, I've got to go. Got a train to catch." He smiled apologetically. "I don't come to London that often these days. It's just my father has a place on Catherine Street that he wants to lease out. I'm running some errands for him. The fire caused quite a lot of havoc."

They paid their bill and headed to the Underground.

A helicopter roamed above them.

"Ugh…urban noises. You don't get much of those in the Fens," Julian complained as he looked up.

A group of secondary school students stirred up a commotion on the elevator; they were excited to see *The Lion King* that night. Their previous viewing had been cancelled because of the fire.

Before they parted, Julian said in a low voice, "Listen, Chance. Perhaps it's not for me to say. I know very well that I shouldn't be the one talking…" Hesitancy danced in his eyes. "After what happened to Isabel, there was some talking. A friend of a friend had stayed a floor below in that accommodation and said that she…Well…there was someone else in her room that night." He cleared his throat. "Just rumours, really."

# A Chinese Remedy

\* \* \*

*An hour later.*

"Do you know why you cannot touch a balloon after peeling oranges?" Felipe asked huskily as he peeled a tangerine.

Chance changed the batteries on his muscle stimulator silently.

"It's because there's a chemical in citrus called limonene. Limonene is a hydrocarbon, and the latex in rubber another. If they meet, they will dissolve in each other, weakening the balloon, so it pops. It's all chemistry, really." Felipe chewed on his fruit. "Isn't it interesting? If you rub a balloon with an orange peel, the balloon explodes. If you rub a deflated balloon on an orange, the orange stays the same."

Chance stood up, storing the used batteries in a dry place.

"Bad mood again?" Felipe asked. "It's a pity that you don't smoke either. Some nice Chesterfields always cheer me up." He sat up, throwing away the fruit peels. "Perhaps we should go out tonight? How does the Duke's Bar sound? Or would you prefer somewhere homier? Bars are great places to meet new people. The other day, I met a linguist who told me that the word 'mummy' means 'sweetheart' in Hebrew. And the word 'man' in Latin is the same as the word 'donkey' in Chechen. Too many choices can indeed overload a man. Isn't it a quandary? At least let's not be Buridan's asses."

Still no response.

Felipe sighed. "Hasn't your mother taught you that it is rude to ignore others? Especially when you are being spoken to?"

"My mother taught me never to talk to strangers."

"Strangers are we now? That's why we make such a good team." Felipe put on his watch. "It's still quite early. Why don't we grab Johnson and eat with

184

him? The kid's been quite helpful lately. It's time for some *nominication*\*."

Dinner was at a place called Vanilla Black.

Johnson fidgeted as they found their table. "Sorry, I don't fancy vegetarian restaurants that much. But there's this girl I've been seeing, and I was hoping to have an idea of this place before asking her out."

Felipe nodded approvingly. "Planning well with simplicity is tough. Do you know about Einstein's approach to problem-solving? I'd say, when you have a clear goal, it's best to spend fifty-five minutes planning and five minutes executing it. As they say, chance favours the prepared mind. Ideas are diamonds; plans are the brilliants. But in my view, plans are worthless, but planning is everything."

They shared a salad of cucumber and seaweed and a plate of baked aubergine and fried mushrooms as Johnson recounted episodes from his Oxford days.

One story that Felipe particularly enjoyed was how people drank wine from their shoes.

"You know." Felipe put down his fork. "If I were ever to go to Oxford. I would choose Kellogg. Because I do love their cereals." He laughed. "And if I were to go to Cambridge. I would go to Hughes Hall, for I've heard they have a good cat."

Johnson went on to tell them how he had once fought on a punt in Cambridge and ended up in the water.

"I'll share one story about my time at Harvard. On the first day of class, the professor told us that we would play a game. The game's called 'StarPower'. I think it'd be more appropriate if it were called 'CapitalPower'. The TA then divided us randomly into three groups: the 'red squares', representing the upper class, another group called the 'blue circles', the middle class, and the last group, the 'green triangles', the lower class. We were given chips as well. They represented the resources, connections, and capital that were endowed with each class. The squares were given thirty, the circles twenty, and the triangles only five." Felipe scratched his chin. "The game was simple. You trade chips to win scores. There are specific scores associated with each threshold of class. The lower classes want to become upper class, while the upper classes want to make rules to retain their privileges. After a twenty-minute round, we found that those who belonged to the circles were still mostly circles, with a few downgrading to the triangles. A few triangles made their way to the circles, but not a single triangle had become a square."

Their dessert came: coconut cake.

They talked a while more about their company and the London Stock Exchange.

After dinner, Felipe told Johnson to have a great night before parting.

They followed a group of tired tourists and found their way to Covent Garden. At eleven o'clock, the Five Guys on Long Acre was packed with drunk diners. They found a window seat.

"Someone said that what we love has three things in common: they are illegal, immoral, or they make you fat. How I miss the Heart Attack Grill. A meal without saturated fats is like a bowdlerised book. I once saw a copy of *Lady Chatterley's Lover* in a library with pages of contents doodled black. Where's the fun of that obscurantism? For an unknowing eye, they might pass it as a confidential file on unlawful killing in Afghanistan from the Pentagon." Felipe lifted a layer of tinfoil wrapper and ate as he said, "I've just eaten five courses at that restaurant, but I feel my stomach's as empty as my savings account." He shook his head. "I'm very disappointed in myself.

Though technically, I'm on a diet that I should have started two years ago."

Chance drank his chocolate milkshake without speaking.

"If I were ever to find work here…No, actually, I would never work here." Felipe scowled from ear to ear as he looked in the direction of the till. "Too noisy, too much shouting and talking. And I can't stand the sight of ketchup."

Chance had found him to be extremely petulant that night.

"French fries, freedom fries*…" Felipe picked up a French fry and popped it into his mouth. "Do you remember the first time you fought someone tooth and nail?" He finished his burger. "I do."

Chance only waited.

"I was fourteen. There was a medical task force coming into the countryside for a reproductive health check-up. Oh! My mother was happy. We didn't have that many opportunities for healthcare services then. Fujimori must have gotten many insights when he went to the UN World Conference on Women in 1995 and…They operated on her…without her consent. It was a sterilisation surgery, and later she died of complications. Do you have any idea how much blood people can lose if a hysterectomy goes wrong? I watched until the last ounce of life left her," he stared at the red checkered tablecloth.

Chance put down his milkshake and listened on.

"*Blood of the Condor* only taught us to stave off the foreigners but not our own. It was the first time that I drew blood," Felipe said as his eyes went distant. "Among all criminals and murderers, the most dangerous type is the criminal physician. Miklos Nyiszli allegedly said this to Josef Mengele at Auschwitz. Medics are a dangerous species of people. They can hurt and heal. And they certainly know how to make people hurt the most – ever heard of Harold Shipman, aka Doctor Death? The only doctor in British medical history to be found guilty of murdering his patients. Do you know what's scary? For every case that's solved, there may be a hundred other unsolved ones. We can save one Sara White, and there are a thousand Saras with their drinks roofied. Sometimes I feel that my mother would not have wanted me to do my current job. She would have been contented enough if I became a tour guide. Or a maca grower. Life was never easy; life was never fair. Was it Kin Hubbard who said that being an optimist after you've got everything you want doesn't count? What will Johnson ever have to worry about? Not having two yachts to rub together and what to put on his LinkedIn, maybe. *A chi troppo, a chi niente.* Some people have it all. If you pay enough money, you could buy your way in as a partner. If you have enough money, you could even outsource a coup d'état. Have you ever heard of the Wonga Coup? Do you know what happened to Margaret Thatcher's son? Another classic project management failure. Anyways, I do take pride in my work. I know someone who works as a social worker in the daytime and a stripper by night – pride in both jobs." He smiled bitterly. "Do you know what my mentor once told me? If you're not at the table, you're on the menu. There's no use dwelling on the past. Perhaps I can celebrate with another Corona, as I have made my way to the circles, or I'd love a milkshake with some of the Devil's buttermilk."

As they left the burger place, their attention was drawn by two people arguing on the roadside. One slapped the other hard, and the other returned the favour. Then they embraced and kissed passionately.

Felipe watched the two with his mouth agape. The scene had left Chance mildly shocked as well.

He remembered.

Alexander Roxborough.

He was the man outside The Horseshoe.

The one Isabel had slapped.

# Chapter 10

The next day, Catherine called. Chance picked up his phone, hesitating. He let the call through in the end.

"Hi. Umm...I'm just calling...one of the motion detector thingies is offline. I'm afraid that Mr Darcy was to blame. He's been rather active since he's lost some weight. I wondered if you could tell me where to find a replacement?"

He thought for a while. "Do you have any engagements later today, Miss Roxborough?"

Catherine laughed. "I've bugger all to do all day. I need to do some job hunting – not my favourite pastime – and some reading as well."

"Then perhaps you could meet me at Leicester Square later? I happen to need to go to the electronics store as well. I'll show you the type you'll need."

"Sounds brilliant."

"Should we say, uh, one? One-thirty?"

"Okay. I'll see you in a bit. Perhaps we could meet under the Swiss Glockenspiel?"

"Very well. I know the place."

He waited until Catherine hung up.

Felipe was out golfing again.

He took the tube to Covent Garden, had lunch in a trattoria in Slingsby

Place, and made his way to Leicester Square.

Catherine was there, kicking her heels under the Glockenspiel. She wore 'KEEP-CALM' T-shirt and beige trousers.

"Good day, Miss Roxborough," he walked up and greeted her. "Been waiting long?"

"No, not at all. I've just spent some time at the Prince Charles Cinema. *Bladerunner* is showing again. Great weather, isn't it?" she said as she put away her *Time Out* magazine.

"Quite nice. Shall we go?"

He led the way, and they arrived at the store a minute later.

He paid for some ink cartridges after he showed her the model she needed.

They walked towards Covent Garden as they talked.

"Miss Roxborough…" He hesitated before taking out a small envelope from his jacket pocket. "Since I'm in no capacity nor position to write you a recommendation letter, I thought that I might as well offer an entry into the field. Consider it an early birthday or a late Easter gift."

He handed her the envelope.

"For me?"

Catherine opened the envelope. It was a gift card for an introductory course on floristry.

"Wow…That's…that's very kind of you, Mr Yang."

"I hope I've spent your forty pounds well." He smiled. "I did have the expenses reimbursed. And I thought it might be better to keep the notes in circulation." He paused. "The staff told me that the meeting point for the course would be at the flower market in New Covent Garden, near Vauxhall…just in case, so you don't get confused with the address of the flower shop. Well…that is if you choose to go."

"Of course, I'll go. It's a…it's such a wonderful opportunity."

She opened her purse and inserted the gift card carefully.

"And I met your uncle the other day," he said. "He told me that he taught at a university in China before."

He had gained this information from Alexander Roxborough's online research profile.

The year he went away was the year after Isabel died.

Felipe once said, when coincidences sound too good to be true, you wonder if they were planned.

"Yes. He liked it there. I visited him once in Xi'an," Catherine mused, "then he moved back because of his last girlfriend." She carried the motion detector in her right hand; it was lighter and cheaper than she had thought. "Although he might seem a composed academic now, when he was younger, he changed partners faster than a juggler juggles. My grandpa once commented that 'Alex himself had singlehandedly facilitated the integration and disintegration of England and Continental Europe'." She gave off a small laugh. "He once had a girlfriend; I still remember her…She was my favourite girlfriend of his, truth to be told. She's such a sentimental person; she cried every time she read me *Don Quixote*'s ending. They had rented a houseboat. That winter was a harsh one. My mother took me to visit them on their boat at Platt's Eyot. They burnt kerosene to keep warm. I didn't like the smell." She stopped suddenly. "Sorry…I was just blathering. I was just like Felipe. He sure can rattle on. And sometimes he speaks so fast… Sometimes I wonder if he always speaks impromptu…"

"No worries. I quite enjoy listening to your childhood episodes."

*Umm…You better mean it.*

"Will you and Felipe stay here for long?" she asked.

He thought for a while. "We leave in late May." He cleared his throat. "Have you known him for long?"

"We met in Thailand. A few years back, Cecil took Sophie and me for a holiday to Phuket. Sophie had lost her luggage, and she had some very important files on her laptop. Felipe helped us to find it."

"I see."

They stopped at a junction.

Catherine took the initiative. "Are you heading back now? I'm heading to Covent Garden to find flying saucers. Do you want to come along? We can have lunch nearby."

"Sorry. I already had mine." He shook his head slightly. "I'm afraid I need to finish some work." He took out his phone and checked. "I think I will take bus 11."

"Bus 11?" Catherine said. "You'll need to wait for it at Trafalgar Square."

He gave her a faint smile. He held up two fingers and made a walking motion. "Bus 11, my version."

"Ah." Catherine smiled too. "That's better. It's better for the environment."

"Goodbye then, Miss Roxborough."

He turned; he busied himself with a new message.

It was from his cousin An. She wrote to tell him that she had received offers from a summer school course at LSE and a postgraduate program in London starting from September. She had arranged to visit in the upcoming May Golden Week holiday to get to know the city.

As he was about to cross the street, something rattled behind him.

"Watch out!" Catherine shouted and grabbed his arm, dragging him back onto the pavement.

A second later, a cyclist whipped past.

Before he had the time to formulate any thanks, he found that he had dropped his phone, and its screen had cracked.

\* \* \*

*The next day.*

The sun had long set when Catherine visited.

"Well, well, look who's here. We don't get so many lovely visitors here," Felipe opened the door and greeted her. "Please, be my guest. Would you like something to drink? Tap water, perhaps?" he joked as he handed her a bottle of Perrier.

She laughed a bit.

"I like it when you laugh, Cathy. You should laugh more. Wear a smile and have friends. Wear a scowl and have wrinkles." Felipe quipped.

Chance was typing on his tablet. "Good evening, Miss Roxborough."

"Please, call me Catherine," she eyed the room. She still wondered why they didn't stay in a hotel. "How are you? And how's your phone?"

"Oh, he's fine, and his phone's fine," Felipe answered for Chance. "What do we have corporate procurement for? We'll get him a new one in no time. Here, let me make some space for you. We don't want you to think that us men can't keep a clean household." Felipe shuffled some papers on the settee. "I was just working on a visa application." He scratched his head. "When I went to Paris the other day, I found out my Schengen visa was about to expire, and although there had been exciting news that Peruvian citizens would soon be able to benefit from a visa-free policy before that. Eh, what a hassle."

Catherine looked at his pen and pencil. "Are you filling those forms out by hand?"

"Yes, I am," Felipe sighed, "that's why they're a pain in the ass."

Catherine wondered, "You haven't got a printer up here?"

"Nope." Felipe went to the kitchen and took out a beer. "I wish we had one. I was trying very hard to make my handwriting legible."

Chance glanced at her and smiled guiltily.

"Why didn't you stay at a hotel?" she asked. "They would have all the business amenities available."

"If we stay in a Hilton or the sorts, the money mostly goes to the multinationals. If we stay in an Airbnb, we benefit the local community truly. Anyway, what's the use of having one? We won't be here for long. In London, I mean," Felipe said.

"Oh. When are you leaving?"

"Late May? Probably around that time. There're still some loose ends to tie up. Boondoggles, really. It's less than a week until International Labour Day, and I still need to work out two merger proposals. That's the sadness of us working class. Did you know that the Spanish word for work, *trabajar*, comes from the Latin word *tripalium*? A three-staked torture device where you tie a subject to it and burn it with fire. And do you know that the International Labour Organisation is the only international institution that has won the Nobel Peace Prize so far? It might come in handy for pub quizzes." Felipe took a sip of his beer. "We salarymen have to go wherever the company needs us to go. And not a single bone in my truck yet. Underpaid, underdressed, and under…the top ones really want to screw us up. You know, to maximise the surplus value and the sorts. " He sat down beside Catherine. "So, Cathy. How's your day? Now that the stalker thing is cleared up. I hope you're having a good time back in the Swinging City and that my assistant did not try to make any ungainly advances towards you."

"Er...well. He has been very helpful and I was at the Prince Charles Cinema earlier."

"I've heard that place started as a cinema that specialised in pornography."

"Umm..." Catherine opened the Perrier and took a sip.

"No comment? I guess I'll take it with a pinch of salt then. And I have heard that they are re-running *Body Heat*. It's my favourite film. Well, if you don't count *Central Station* or *The Ladykillers* or *In the Mood for Love*, that is. Did you know that Kathleen Turner had studied in London? My favourite line from that film is 'every time you try a decent crime, and there are fifty ways to fuck up'. Excuse me for the uncouth language. I sometimes wonder if a merger is not unlike a murder. One miscalculation could foil a good plan. Like Quaker Oats, like Time Warner. Life is indeed a box of chocolates." Felipe winced. "And did you have popcorn? Sweet or salty?"

"Sea salt isn't bad. I had a deal on the sweet." She smiled.

"Such a silly girl. Deals are not companies being nice to you; they just want to price discriminate you. And crisps are only cancer cells presented in nice packages." Felipe shot a look at Chance. "Did you know that he likes to drink his tea with salt? Isn't he a stickler of peculiarity?"

Catherine laughed a little. "Well...we can accommodate a little diversity in taste."

"Like people say, *de gustibus non disputandum est*. There's no accounting for taste. And yes. I do believe that the UK is very good at being accommodating...and very selective as well." Felipe finished his beer. "You know, I had to apply for a British visa before. They asked some earnest questions about my background. 'Have you ever been arrested and charged with any offence?' 'Have you ever expressed views that...may glorify and justify terrorist violence?' 'Have you ever been involved in any activities against humanity?' and 'Have you engaged in any other activities that might indicate that you may not be' – how did they put it? Ah, that 'you may not be considered a person of good character?'" Felipe grinned. "You know, with such a rigid system, I do sometimes wonder how Pinochet slipped into London. Someone must have neglected their duties. Or do you suppose they let him into the pen so they could shut the door behind him? As they say, every door may be shut but death's door."

He picked up the papers and put them inside a manila envelope. "Now, if you'll excuse me, I have a previous engagement. A friend had promised me a night at a casino. I would rather prefer another experience – not that I want to look a gift horse in the mouth. But tonight is serious business like pulling teeth." Felipe checked his Daytona. "*Joder!* I'm already running late! The trouble with being punctual is that there's nobody to appreciate it. The benefit of being late is that it enhances my authority. Perhaps I'll leave you two for dinner." He looked at Chance. "Can I trust you to see her home?"

Felipe turned back and smiled. "Cathy. You are the equestrian here. I haven't seen much of a horse's mouth. But I used to work with cows and alpacas. Believe me; you wouldn't want to get close to their mouths."

\* \* \*

*An hour later.*

Felipe followed Johnson into the Ritz Club.

"What a gorgeous place!" he exclaimed as he adjusted his tux. "This looks exactly like the *Casino Royale* in my imagination."

"When they redecorated this place, they used six thousand books of gold leaf," Johnson explained. "Johnny Depp and the Clintons are regulars.

Never met them, though. But no one could escape the charm of a Louis XVI-styled place like this."

"You know, kid. I've witnessed many occasions where contracts worth billions were sealed over dinner. But the hard part was getting yourself a place at the table."

Felipe looked around, taking in the opulent decorations, the high ceilings, the chandelier, the crimson velvet carpets, and the golden mise-en-scène.

There were paintings on the wall of blue skies and white clouds. Under them, the London circles talked, joked, and laughed.

"Mr Kazama, would you like to have dinner first?" Johnson inquired as he pointed to some curtains at the far end of the room.

"Yes, why not? After all, this is an evening to celebrate, and I'm determined to exercise some of my panache." Felipe smiled thoughtfully as he loosened his bow tie. "Now, if I were to be picky or to find quarrel in a straw, as you might say, this place is grand, but it does seem rather compact in measures as a casino. Of course, I may be speaking as someone who has had more dealings in Vegas-style facilities."

"Yes. There is a discreet rule that the hotel does not encourage people to gamble other than to provide a relaxing atmosphere."

"Oh, Johnny." A middle-aged man stood up at a nearby table. He was overly excited. "Fancy seeing you here. Sylvia and I are in town to visit a friend. We were just speaking of you. What a lovely surprise!"

Johnson introduced them. "Mr Kazama. This is my brother-in-law, Henry Dowland. He is with the Crown Estate." He hesitated. "Perhaps…"

"No worries," Felipe said. "You go have your fun, and I'll have mine."

Johnson nodded happily.

Felipe roamed around. He watched a young man trying and failing his luck at Baccarat. He wore a custom-made Zegna suit and an H. Moser & Cie. He rubbed his thick knuckles whenever the goddess of fortune ran against his favour. Felipe followed him to the bar and sat down with an empty seat between them.

"Having a good time?" Felipe asked casually as he nurtured his whiskey.

"Can't say it's my best."

"You know–" Felipe leaned closer– "I've been told that reading books is forbidden in casinos in Macau, as the term sounds similar to losing." He put down his drink. "But if it's true, how long is it before one must stop reading? A day, a week? A life, maybe?"

The young man chuckled. "Oh, the Chinese are quite superstitious. You should never gift them any watches or clockwork because it rhymes with death."

"Quite right." Felipe smiled. "I have a friend who refuses to share a pear with anyone because the act sounds similar to 'to separate' in Mandarin." He thought for a while. "And it's not only the Chinese. In Japan, during business negotiations, people would never dare to drink too much tea or coffee because they believe fortune will slip away if they pass water often."

The other man laughed. "So, if you want to hold the better end of a bargain, why not serve a lot of drinks to the other company?"

"Unfortunately, that is the common practice. I wonder why people believe in superstitions. After all, we live in a world with manufactured risks." He looked in the direction of the casino. "Do you know what the odds are of a chandelier falling and killing the crowd below? Black swans may not be so rare after all." Felipe sipped his drink again. "Talking about drinking…I wonder if you could enlighten me on one issue."

"Sure."

"Do you drink often?"

"Well, I consider myself an *omnivore* when it comes to alcohol."

"Some liquid courage in happy hours would not harm." Felipe grinned. "To loosen the lips, the teeth, and the tip of the tongue."

"What business are you in? If you don't mind me asking?"

"Oh, I don't mind at all. I do the boring stuff, M&A. You know the sorts. Finance is a lovely field that makes me want to say the f-word. No one really loves finance; they just love everything associated with the money."

"Heard it's good money. My pa's company recently completed a delicate financial manoeuvre. They borrowed money to make a lot of money. He only golfs these days."

Felipe smiled as he downed his drink. "Someone said that money couldn't buy us friends, but at least it can make you meet better-quality enemies. I'd say that money certainly helps you to open doors..." He grinned again. "And to close some for others."

He pulled out his cigar case. "Care for one?"

"Thanks, I'll pass." The young man shook his head. "I've switched to vaping. It's supposed to be better for your health."

"I'm still old-school." Felipe smiled. "Who knows what damage e-cigarettes might do? Look at the public health policymaking of today," he snorted. "It's okay to bombard people with messages to have their five-a-day, but unacceptable if smokers want to have some genuine smoking experiences. Did you know the word 'cigar' originally comes from Mayan and 'cocaine' comes from Quechua? And did you know that Japan Tobacco had procured a new building right by the WHO headquarters in Geneva in the interest of protecting the rights of the world's vast number of smokers? I'll tell you what. When I'm back, I think I might play as well. *Chemin de fer.* I believe there's something called gamesmanship. Somehow I feel I might win tonight." He grinned. "Sometimes I like to watch, but other times I like to take part, especially if there's money to be made. I'm no piker tonight." Felipe stood up and sauntered out of the room.

\* \* \*

It was well past midnight when Chance got back to his temporary residence at Oval.

Felipe was already back. He was reading under dim light.

He read out loud as Chance washed his hands.

"'His eyes were like tunnels; my first thought was that he had committed a crime\*.'"

When Chance re-emerged from the bathroom, Felipe closed his book.

"How was dinner?"

"It was fine. We went to Vanilla Black."

"Isn't she a bit of a smasher? Did you see her home?"

"Yes."

"Is that a 'yes' to my first question or my second? Never mind. I love to walk on the streets of Beijing and Tokyo late at night. Even without my leather sap. But it's never that safe in London or the Big Apple."

Felipe picked up his phone and turned on the radio app he liked.

A song was halfway through. It was 'Cathy' by Tohyama Hitomi.

"How fitting," Felipe put down his book. "I've had a most tiresome day. I called Sara earlier."

Chance waited.

"I thought that if she insisted on giving me the silent treatment, I might as well pursue her with a proactive approach to quench that *douleur exquise* of mine. I told her that *j'ai le cafard*, and she has always been my favourite cucumber sandwich on the lawn. Then I asked if I could come around later. She said it was not good timing because her Aunt Flo had come to visit."

Chance continued to listen, but his ears were more attuned to the song than Felipe's recounting.

"I told her not to sweat because my motto is family first. I told her that I'd be delighted to meet her aunt. We could show her around tomorrow and have tea together at Harrods. Then she hung up on me. After a cursory search, I understood why. She must think that I am the most uncaring, dim-witted, two-legged man-imal on Earth."

The song ended. Felipe turned off the radio app.

"I was just earnest and sincere. I was as eager to meet Sara's aunt as I would look forward to meeting your stepmother." He smiled. "I'm not a well-read person, but I do like to read a little in my spare time, from sonnets to thrillers. And the last time that I read a book with a menstruating protagonist was in *1Q84*."

His left hand went under his chin. "If children can't be what they can't see, how can they grasp the gravity of a natural part of human's daily existence if they don't read it in books? Don't see it on TV? If we all speak in riddles, how are we ever to learn?"

Felipe stood up and removed his bowtie.

"Perhaps we should propose a fund for a cultural pledge, that whenever writers write a new book, they include at least one menstruating character to avoid the embarrassment…the turmoil that I'm feeling now."

# Chapter 11

**Late May**

*When the copper railings outside Oxford Circus Station are hot to touch, you know that summer has come to London,* Catherine thought as she walked out of the floristry academy at Slingsby Place and found her way to the Royal Opera House.

The sun did not shy away that day.

Covent Garden was filled with children who hummed the tunes of *Matilda the Musical.*

She checked her phone; there was still time before the opening of *La Bohème.* Her uncle and his date should be here soon. An older lady passed holding a tussie-mussie of asters from the flower academy. Catherine watched as the lady disappeared around the street corner.

*Practice makes perfect…*

She looked at her hands. There were various cuts and scratches. The life of a tyro florist was never easy, but it had its appeal.

*Thanks to…*

Catherine had not seen the person in question since their night at that vegetarian place near Chancery Lane.

She had had a great birthday with Mick, her uncle, and Cecil. Mr Darcy's diet programme had been a success. And she had even found fresh flying saucers with crunchy fillings last week.

*But something was amiss…*

She had often wondered why he was called Chance. She wondered what the odds of running into a friend at Covent Garden were.

A cluster of opera-goers had gathered. There was still no sign of her uncle or Valerie.

Someone caught her eye as she searched for them.

*It's him!*

She wanted to call out but then saw someone at his side. A svelte Asian girl held onto his right arm as they laughed and talked. She looked chipper and wore a long gambier-dyed silk dress with a fine ribboned straw hat.

*It's really him.*

Catherine rummaged through her bag, trying to find her sunglasses.

But she was too late.

"Good evening, Miss Roxborough. How have you been?" He held his date's arm.

"Hi. I'm well. It's been a while." She faked a smile. "I thought that you and Felipe had already left the country."

"Something delayed us." He paused. "I will not go without saying goodbye."

"Nice to meet you." The girl beside him reached out her hand. "My name is An, spelt A N. I have to say…you have such beautiful earrings."

"Very nice earrings indeed," he smirked knowingly.

"Oh, thank you. If you're interested, I'm sure he knows where to get a pair for you."

*As well*, Catherine thought as she touched the bee earrings.

"If you will allow me to introduce–" he looked her in the eyes– "An is my cousin."

*Oh.* Catherine let out the breath that she'd been holding. "Very nice meeting you. I'm Catherine. I hope you're enjoying London?"

"Yes. It's my first time in London, and the first time at an opera as well. I wanted to visit during our Golden Week holiday, but it was a lot cheaper to travel off-season. Ha, ha. I didn't know that there were so many pedestrian walks paved with stones," An said as pain crossed her face. "My heels are killing me. I'll know to pack some flats when I come again in July."

Catherine could identify with her. "Heels always give me trouble as well. Try to tape your middle toes. It might reduce the pain."

"Yeah. I will try it for sure."

"Cathy? I have your ticket here," someone called behind her.

Catherine turned back. Her uncle and Valerie were there.

"Lovely weather, isn't it?" Alexander Roxborough greeted them.

They exchanged pleasantries and parted to find their seats.

After the performance, it took them some twenty minutes to collect their bags and umbrellas. No one wanted a heavy meal after seeing the tragic romance, so they settled at the tea area at Ladurée.

"Did you know that *La Bohème* was first performed in Covent Garden in 1897?"

Valerie told some stories of Puccini's early days. Alexander Roxborough shared his time teaching in China. An asked some questions and answered some more. Chance had ordered a rose-petal sorbet for dessert. He frowned as he tasted it.

"Do you not like it?" Catherine asked as she watched him.

"No." He smiled faintly. "It's quite nice." He paused. "I remembered someone…I wondered if that person liked it or not."

Catherine arranged her napkin, "I haven't told you yet. I've completed the introductory course at the flower academy. It's a very rewarding experience. I'm taking a longer course now."

"That's nice to know." He smiled. "I might pop in one day to get some white roses – you know, to celebrate new beginnings for a friend."

As they prepare to leave, An's straw hat dropped onto the floor. Catherine bent down to retrieve it, and Chance bent down as well. Their fingers touched for a moment.

She felt as if she had eaten a pack of flying saucers.

"Sorry. Thank you." He took the hat and looked away.

An was staying at the Holiday Inn in Bloomsbury. Catherine's uncle lived with Valerie near Russell Square. The five of them conversed more as they walked in that direction. The ladies were happily discussing a Sonia Delaunay exhibition at the Tate Modern and Bob the Street Cat.

"Professor Roxborough." Chance slowed down. "Would you take offence if I asked you a personal question?"

"Is it about Isabel?"

"Yes."

"I failed her as her father," Alexander Roxborough deliberated. "I met her mother when she came to London as an exchange student. Communication back then was not as quick and as developed as today. She was from a pious Catholic family. I only knew after Isabel was born. Isabel was furious at me for not being there for her mother and her."

They stopped at a junction, and Alexander Roxborough lowered his voice. "The night she…Cecil told me that the law faculty were having an event. I went to see her, to ask for her forgiveness again, but she was not there. She had left early because a woman took her child there, and the child had tried to touch a balloon after peeling an orange. Isabel stopped the child, but the mother was angry because she thought she was reprimanding her child for no reason."

"I have some information that she might…that there was someone in her room that night."

"A friend of mine worked in the Vice Unit at the time. We had a person in mind, but never enough evidence. Sometime later, we learnt that someone had spilt the beans."

"I could help you find this person, whoever it might be."

"There is no longer the need," Alexander Roxborough sighed. "I heard that he went missing on a hunting trip to Belarus recently. The local authorities found his watch covered in blood by a creek. They concluded that the…chances that he survived were slim."

"Does…does Catherine know of Isabel?"

"No."

"Do you…do you perhaps wish to tell her?"

"No." The professor hesitated. "I believe it is for the best if neither of us does."

"Then, I will not."

They were nearing An's hotel. She turned to say goodnight.

"I do believe in karma," Alexander Roxborough said before they parted. "If he had called an ambulance, she could have been saved."

Later, Chance went down to the Underground platform with Catherine.

"Miss Roxborough, I was wondering if I could see you home again?" He gave a faint smile. "I've heard the London streets are not quite as…safe as they appear, especially at night."

\* \* \*

*The next day.*

Felipe had stayed at Sara's.

Chance slept in, had a shower, shaved, and made a chicken sandwich. Then he ran some searches on his tablet as he ate.

There was indeed a news article on a missing person: a British national who had gone missing on a leisure trip to Belarus in early May. As well as his watch, the police had found a pack of nicotine gum not far from his tent.

A young, promising solicitor…

When he saw the missing solicitor's last name, he dared not make an association.

Someone knocked just as he was checking for more information.

He closed his tablet, got up, and opened the door.

Johnson was there. He was wearing a white shirt with wet patches under his arms.

"Chance, is this your cousin?" Johnson asked as An crept up the stairs.

Her hair was dishevelled, and her elbows grazed.

"What happened?" he asked in Chinese.

An gave him a sour face. "I was walking here, and someone cat-called me. I was so angry that I tried to give him a lesson." She switched to English. "This gentleman here helped me. He said he is your colleague." An washed her elbow wounds at the sink. "Remind me when I come again, to bring some dry chilli powder and make some extra hot chilli pepper spray."

Chance helped her to disinfect the wounds as Johnson re-stocked their fridge.

"I used to get very bad road-rashes," Johnson put in cans of beer and mineral water. "Ugh, this fridge smells a lot better now. Before you came, Mr Kazama lived on takeaway curries. He even took notes that this curry house didn't use authentic nutmeg or good turmeric. They all taste the same to me, though."

Chance thanked Johnson for the opera tickets. After An had had time to collect herself, he decided to spend the afternoon with his cousin.

They took the tube to Embankment and walked along Victoria Embankment Gardens.

"Ah! Sneakers are so comfortable to walk in!" An stretched her legs. "Did you know that a writer could describe the London rain with more than two hundred similes and metaphors? I've been here a week, and I have yet to experience a rainy London."

They sat on a bench and watched two children blow bubbles nearby.

"Other than your pepper spray, bring a sturdy umbrella. You will need it. Trust me."

"I still remember when we watched re-runs of *Erma* as kids. You remember, right? The show based on Lao She's book *Mr Ma & Son*. Did you know that they filmed a lot of the London scenes in Qingdao? Only the part where you can see St Paul's Cathedral was filmed here."

He had remembered that story; it was a sad one.

An older Asian man hurried down the road and moved towards them. He looked as if a spirit were chasing him.

"*Due u si bik…Chanis?*" he asked with a ragged voice.

An smiled and replied in Chinese, "Yes!"

The man took a deep breath. "Great! I asked down the way and finally found someone!" He cleared his throat. "I'm supposed to meet my daughter and son-in-law at a place around here." He was anxious, and his eyes blinked fast. "It's a theatre…something about mothers."

Chance thought for a while and gave him detailed directions to the Novello Theatre.

"Remember when we couldn't even say directions in English?" An mused. "Hard work pays off. I only had to take the IELTS once."

They started to walk again as An talked about her plans. "I'm thinking about renting a room or sharing with someone. There are many things to decide. Which telecom company to use, for example. I got a free SIM card with the in-flight magazine with one-pound credit. But I've heard that Vodafone's signal is better, and you can use its WiFi on the Underground, but I already used that number to register for some school services, and it's too much work to change it."

He thought for a while. "You can transfer your number to another network."

"How long does it take?"

"From what I know, about three to four working days."

"Then I'll try. It's worth trying." An winced. "Oh, I had blisters from the heels. I need to find a pharmacy and get some anti-blister stick for my poor feet."

They found a pharmacy around the corner.

He spotted a familiar figure as An compared the prices of footcare products.

"Good day, Mrs Wurman." He walked to the prescription counter.

"Oh." Tilly had recognised him. "Need any help? Your friend has been considering her choices for some time."

"She's fine. Thank you." He paused. "Heard that you're moving house."

"News travels fast." Tilly smiled. "Yes. I'll end my rotation here by the end of the month. Then we'll go."

He turned around. An was still deciding.

"If you don't mind me asking – what made you want to become a pharmacist?"

"The short answer is that I never had the grades to become a medic. The long answer is that I was abandoned because I had a heart defect. When my parents adopted me, a pharmacist at our community health centre offered us a lot of help and support."

She glanced in An's direction. "Is she your…"

"She's my sister. Cousin, actually."

"Are you a one-child?"

"Yes."

"And she?"

"She's an only daughter."

Tilly lowered her eyes. "I hope her parents treated her well."

He decided to change the topic. "Will you miss your job?"

"Most likely." Tilly thought as she straightened her white coat. "It's a waste to let all the years of training go. I had a lot of fun with the job." She gave a small laugh. "I once had a customer who told me she wanted to buy Sildenafil. Her husband told her it was a nutritional supplement. But I couldn't say. Really. China sounds so distant, and I only know it from books and films. I certainly did not realise that Shanghai alone is four times the size of London. Perhaps I could make myself useful there, like volunteering to teach English. But I know what I want to do. I'll go and see the pandas in Chengdu and have some genuine Sichuan hotpots."

"Do you like spicy food?"

"Yes. Very much. But Joyce did not." She thought for a while. "She would only order 'mild' at Nando's." She looked at him with unease. "If there's nothing else that I can help you with…"

"Is it possible to buy replacement pads for electric muscle stimulators here?"

"Sure. Let me check for you." Tilly ran some searches on a desktop computer. "Seems you can only click and collect."

"Thank you, Mrs Wurman. That would be fine," he said, "and I hope you enjoy your new life."

An had paid for her anti-blister stick. She wanted to head back to her hotel as the time difference was still making her dizzy.

They bought some fruits, snacks, and mineral water at a nearby Sainsbury's, and he saw her to her room. When he got to the hotel lobby, someone had called – a number he didn't recognise.

He connected the call.

"Hello, is this Mr Chang-zi Yang? My name is Dean Tellier, and I'm a staff member at the National Gallery. We have Miss Catherine Roxborough here. She fell down the steps in front of the Gallery. It was a minor injury, but unfortunately, her phone is no longer functioning. She wanted us to contact you."

Everything went quiet around him.

Another call cut in; it was Felipe.

Chance could hear the sounds of helicopters.

"Hey, buddy. I'm in Rochester now. It's a beautiful place. Didn't fail its name. Visiting Sara's parents and finally meeting her aunt. A very nice lady who likes to collect buttons. Don't worry about me. Take your time. I may or may not head back today."

The call ended.

"Hello? Are you still there? Mr Yang?" the other end of the phone urged.

He had no time to think.

# Chapter 12

He made it to Trafalgar Square in under ten minutes. By the time he arrived, his ribs had hurt wildly from the running.

A helicopter hovered above the area. Its sound did not bode too well with the 'Auld Lang Syne' someone played on bagpipes by the fountain.

Catherine sat barefoot on the stone steps in front of the National Gallery, looking at the street performers and groups of tourists. She looked like a cat who had fallen into a well.

"Miss Roxborough? Are you okay?" He eyed the area and approached her. "Would you like to go to your GP?"

She looked up. "No. I'm quite alright. I only turned my ankle slightly. Nothing that I won't live through."

He wanted to stop her from saying these words. He knew better than to talk about life and death with all seriousness.

"Only my phone is a lost cause now, and I didn't have the foresight to memorise Cecil's or my uncle's number. I had your card…"

"Can I have a look?"

"Y…yes." Catherine lifted her trouser leg gently.

He rubbed his hands. "My hands are a bit cold, sorry."

He sat beside her and examined her right foot. Her ankle had swollen up. A staff member from the National Gallery emerged. He brought a cup of ice from a café inside. The makeshift ice pack served its purpose well.

Chance helped Catherine up, gathered her bag and shoes, thanked the man, and hailed a cab.

"I was quite certain that someone bumped into me. Never mind. I'll watch where I'm going next time," she murmured and leaned towards the door side as he held the ice cup on her ankle.

*His hands were quite warm...Now they must be cold*, she thought.

"I can take it from here." She reached her hand down.

"Stay still, Miss Roxborough," he wiped a thin layer of water from the cup's surface.

*Still Miss Roxborough...*

Catherine closed her eyes and felt the coldness.

They arrived at her house. He paid for the cab with cash and helped her inside.

Mr Darcy meowed anxiously around them.

"Would you mind if I borrowed your keys?" he asked as he helped her recline on a lounge chair in the living room.

"Umm...fine. Just don't let Mr Darcy out...or near you."

He smiled ruefully. "That's ok. At least I know where the Band-Aids are."

He was gone for ten minutes or so.

Catherine winced, half-lying on the chair. One side of her hip hurt terribly; it could well develop a bruise by tomorrow.

She limped across the room to get some unfinished reading for distraction. By the time he was back, she knew there was no need to hide the book.

He bought her some fruits, pots of hummus with veggie sticks, and some gluten-free bread.

Later, he made her a glass of kale juice as she called Cecil, who agreed to stop by an electronics store on his way home.

"Now, Miss Roxborough," he said, "I'd better get going. There's still some unfinished business." He smiled faintly. "Please take care. Could I perhaps call on you tomorrow?"

Catherine thanked him and held Mr Darcy close to her heart as the door shut.

\* \* \*

*An hour later.*

He jumped the stairs two at a time, found his keys, and opened the door.

Felipe was back. He was sitting in a bespoke suit on the settee with his legs crossed.

"Tupí or not Tupí? That's the Whites' burden*," Felipe stretched his arms and put his hands behind his neck. "Sara's parents did not quite enjoy my discussions of the traditional Brazilian culinary practices during lunch. I haven't even brought up my favourite *otsumami** yet. I do miss Japanese dining. Who wouldn't want some nice soy sauce *inagos** on Koshihikari rice?" He let out a breath. "But her nephew did show some interest. I'm thinking of sending him a gift for Children's Day on 1st June. Would you say that childhood is a human invention and capitalism concerns converting wants into needs? What do you think? Perhaps a teddy bear? And a card. What shall I write? How about: 'greetings from Minsk*'?" He curled his lips and singsonged. "I think better not. I hate to bring geopolitics into everyday life. Not when I'm enjoying the hospitality of London this much. How does a drone sound? Difficult choices, really. Even a three-year-old might be tempted to hurl unbidden cargo into the neighbour's backyard."

Chance shut the door forcefully, almost breaking the hinge.

"Now, now, that was uncalled for. We could do with a little more love and peace in this house…" Felipe gave him a look. "Or the neighbours might complain about the noise again. Not that we make that much, but imagination does run wild. They must be thinking that we love to smoke both ends of the cigar and drink from the Warren Cup."

"Catherine fell off the steps at the National Gallery this afternoon."

"Poor Cathy, she really needs to mind that gap, so to speak. I take it that you went to her rescue again? Always suffering from the Sir Galahad Complex?" Felipe smiled. "Coming back to my problem at hand…How about a 3D printer for a gift? Or an iPhone? The latest model? What do people toy with these days?"

"It was you, wasn't it?"

Felipe lowered his eyes. "I beg your pardon?"

"You know *bloody* well what I mean."

"Do enlighten me on the issue." Felipe stood up and walked to the window. "An Arabian proverb says that six things may know a fool: anger without cause, speech without profit, change without progress, inquiry without object, putting trust in a stranger, and mistaking foes for friends."

Chance inhaled deeply, and then his restraint collapsed.

He grabbed Felipe by his crisp collar, shovelled him onto the wall, and punched him low in the abdomen.

"*Señor, por favor!*" Felipe pleaded. "Do not wrinkle my Brioni."

Chance punched him again. "I heard a helicopter on your call, and there were no helicopters scheduled over Rochester today!"

"Good to know that you paid attention to…certain details." Felipe smiled. "And you didn't hold your thumb inside your fist."

"How dare you hurt her!"

"Aren't you grateful that I helped to move things forward? A little catalysing…bonding…where the rubber meets the road? And she's a lot stronger than you think. You're doing her an injustice, thinking that she's a damsel in distress." Felipe smiled again. "And one more piece of advice from a mentor. Next time, if someone gifts an electronic device, you better weigh it against the official specs."

He choked Felipe's throat.

"Never say that…I never gave you any hints. I gave you…more leads than…the amount of cat h…air on your back…side," Felipe panted.

Chance swatted him again. "I had my first fight when I was twelve. I lost that time. And I promised myself that I would never get into another. And if I ever did," he growled, "I would show no leniency!"

"I do admire your spirit. Did you know that tango evolved from duelling postures?" Felipe sucked his gum. "If you're thinking about that taser, think again." He grinned.

Chance searched his jacket pocket with one hand; it was empty.

"Guess who's got it now?" Felipe smiled as his strong hands clawed Chance's wrists. "I must talk with Sidney…you could do with some help on tactics-"

Someone knocked – a tentative knock at first, which became more insistent.

"Now, if you'll excuse me." Felipe pushed Chance aside and rearranged his tie.

He opened the door.

It was the prim lady without her dog. She looked gaunter.

"Umm…I heard some noises. I wondered…" she said timidly.

Felipe laughed facetiously. "Oh! Mrs Turill, I'm so sorry to have disturbed you. My buddy and I have been playing a game. Just a little rough play… We may have taken it too far. Would you care to join us? It's called 'circles, triangles, and squares'. It's a fun game where cheating, lying, and blagging are allowed…even encouraged."

"I better not. I need my walk in the park. Please keep your voices down."

"Will do."

Felipe bowed slightly, closed the door, and turned back to Chance.

"I've scratched your back. Now you better scratch mine. You came here to do a job. No more dilly-dallying. Don't pass Go, and you can collect your two hundred dollars later."

* * *

*The next day.*

Catherine limped to the door as the bell rang.

"Evening, Miss Roxborough."

He carried a paper bag in one hand, in it a small bouquet of white roses, and some envelopes in the other. "Are you feeling better today? Here's your mail."

"Yes. I've been using ice packs. The swelling is not so bad," Catherine fetched her mail and had a quick look through. There was a new issue of *Granta*. Besides that, nothing exciting or useful.

He helped her into the house and put the paper bag down on the table. "I've brought something that might help," he tore the wrapper off a bottle of vodka.

Catherine eyed him suspiciously. "Isn't it a bit early for nightcaps, Mr Yang?"

"It's not for drinking." He smiled as he took out the white roses and arranged them in a glass vase. "I came to say goodbye. I'm flying out tonight."

*Oh.*

Even Mr Darcy fell silent.

Catherine collected herself. "Such a pity that you didn't get to enjoy London in the summer."

He looked away as he took out a paperback from the bag. "I've noticed the progress of your bookmark. Here's the sequel to pass some time. Forgive me for taking liberties and not keeping things to myself."

"No. It's fine." Catherine tilted her chin up. "It's a good read."

"I'll put it here."

He put down the book and brought a dining chair to the living room, besides Catherine's lounge chair. "Now for the exciting bit…" He went to the kitchen again and retrieved a small bowl.

Catherine and Mr Darcy watched him as he took off his jacket, rolled up his shirt sleeves, opened the vodka, poured some out into the porcelain bowl, and ignited the liquid with a lighter. A pale blue fire danced.

Mr Darcy ran up to investigate and whooshed away when his whiskers touched the flame.

"If I may." He sat down on the chair and gently lifted her leg. "It's a remedy my grandmother used when I fell from a tree once."

Catherine could not help but laugh. "From a tree?"

"Yes. Some wasps attacked me; I believe." He removed her sock. "Don't worry. I promise it won't hurt. It helps to alleviate the bruising and pain."

He smiled. "But it should only be applied twenty-four hours after the initial injury."

He dipped his hand into the bowl and scooped some blue fire onto his palm. He held it carefully and rubbed it quickly on Catherine's ankle.

She watched as that patch of skin reddened. And she felt her cheeks flush.

*Oh my.*

A warmth flowed through her ankle, and the fire was not as hot as she had imagined.

*Like roasting marshmallows around a campfire on a winter day…*

Mr Darcy observed this mysterious ritual from afar.

A few minutes passed, and neither spoke.

When the fire had burnt clean, Catherine asked, "Why are you called 'Chance'?" She paused. "To be fair, my parents named me after my great-grandmother on my mother's side."

He looked up but did not stop his ministrations. "It sounds similar enough to my Chinese name. When I first went to the US, I watched a film. It was a very educational one."

"What was it called?"

"*Being There.* The protagonist was called Chance. I understood it even though my English was very poor."

His hands stopped. "My grandmother used to perform another cure on me whenever I had a cold. She would use a clean needle and let some blood out of my fingers. It worked."

"Oh." Catherine tilted her head. "That sounds…I better not catch a cold."

"Good." He put her sock back on and closed the cap on the vodka. "And never attempt this when unsupervised. Well…" He checked his watch. "I should get going."

Catherine sat up. "And what does your Chinese name mean?"

He smiled. "Perhaps I will tell you the next time we meet." He stood up. "There are some Epsom salts, fresh rosemary, and soya milk in that bag as well. I've heard that soaking in them is good to ease the bruising. Perhaps you could try later tonight."

He looked at her. "Miss Roxborough, is there anything else that I could do for you?"

*Yeah. I have one more bruise needing attention…*

Catherine shook her head slightly, "Thank you, Mr Yang. You've been most kind and very helpful."

He looked in the direction of the kitchen. "Do you want me to take out your garbage for you?"

"No."

*Rubbish! Talk! Now!*

Catherine got up from the lounge chair. "I hope you have a nice flight. I will…see you out."

*Stop. Stop him right now.*

She walked him to the door.

"Goodbye, then."

"Goodbye."

He turned, and the door closed behind him.

*To say goodbye is hoping to live,* he thought as he opened his umbrella.

Catherine and Mr Darcy hid behind the curtains and watched him walking away.

*Away…*

*Far away…*

# CHAPTER 13

**F our weeks later**

July in Shanghai was like a Turkish bath. Unlike the scorching heat of Europe, the whole city was steaming. The cicadas rested and sang staccato as the sweat of passers-by evaporated into clouds, soaring over the metropolis.

The heat did not put off the shoppers who bustled around the numerous boutiques and luxury malls lined on West Nanjing Road and the alleys behind. High-voltage power lines crisscrossed the wax-paper sky in hash keys, overlooking dense vegetation below.

Chance and Felipe emerged from a lane not far from the Jing'an Temple. A police officer blew his whistle, warning them not to jaywalk.

"Speaking of famous Shanghai dishes…" Felipe held a paper takeaway box in his hand. "One must try xiaolongbao and…" He took a freshly baked savoury pork mooncake and had a bite. "It pains me to remember how I guzzled the so-called 'buns' in London restaurants."

Chance did not answer as the two of them passed several boutique stores and stopped at a hotel entrance. The revolving door greeted them with gushes of cold air.

They entered the lobby. It was as cool as a fjord. The General Manager

greeted them. He thanked them for choosing to stay at the hotel for such
a long time.

Felipe shrugged. "You know. I've had plenty of opportunities to stay at
niche, luxury hotels by the fashion and jewellery brands. They only know
how to send their visitors away with some cheap, faux leather luggage tags.
When it comes to hospitality, my experience tells me that it's always better
to leave things to the professionals."

Goosebumps stood on Chance's arms as he took out his room key and
headed to the lift.

A familiar logo of the crown and the lion on the crimson carpet
welcomed them as they stepped in.

Felipe leaned against the handrail and continued to savour his mooncakes.

A minute later, they returned to their penthouse suite with its view of
the Oriental Pearl Tower.

The décor in the room reminded Chance of a film set in Shanghai under
Japanese occupation during World War Two. It had a lavish dining area
big enough to seat ten.

Felipe dumped his takeaway box in the trash, cleaned his fingers with a
napkin, turned on the TV, and collapsed on the couch.

A golf commentator's voice came on.

Chance checked his phone. There was a message from his cousin An.
She had already rented an apartment near Shakespeare's Globe and had
met up with a few classmates-to-be.

"Let me find the Blatantly Blithering Company. It's only been a month,
but I kinda miss the British accent." Felipe yawned.

Two hours later, they were ready.

They ventured downstairs without too much conversation and made their way to a nearby Japanese restaurant as Felipe had already grown tired of the hotel's offerings.

"The concept of *wagyu* is so overrated; perhaps I should consider retiring to Hokkaido and opening a farm there," said Felipe as he ate diced beef served on reed leaves. "Someone I know from Nomura went to start a craft brewery in Kyoto."

Chance didn't say anything.

"Perhaps I should have signed you up for some anger management and mindfulness courses. The human body is a system. Inputs and outputs. You should have more dissipated habits. All your pent-up anger has no place to go; it could lead to either internal destruction or external damage. Someone I know has a smart way of dealing with his anger. Whenever he quarrels with his wife, he goes out and drives for Uber, so he can stay away from her and make money at the same time. You are quite a slugger. You know, I should be glad that you didn't give me a shiner. A man has his stature to consider."

After dinner, they made their way to another established five-star hotel nearby.

It had a lobby crowded with tourists and travellers. Chance sat on the communal sofa and checked the time; it was almost seven.

The sun that had hidden all day decided to show up, leaving wisps of lotus-root-coloured clouds.

"See you later, alligator." Felipe smiled at him and strolled away.

Seven o'clock. Chance stood up and walked towards the hotel's front door.

A minibus parked not far away. A few ladies came down as they chitchatted. He quickly walked past the bus, then halted, turned, and asked in a voice neither too loud to disturb nor too small to go unnoticed, "Mrs Wurman?"

A figure in a light-coloured *qipao* stopped. She turned around with question marks on her face.

"Small world." He feigned surprise. "Or should I say...small Shanghai?"

"Oh." Tilly laughed. "I do believe in fate." She clutched her handbag. "As they say, once is happenstance and twice is a coincidence."

"Are you enjoying your new life in Shanghai? Have you visited Sichuan yet?" he asked.

"Life is treating me well." Tilly nodded. "I've been learning Mandarin. My teacher always applauds my pronunciation. It seems like some things are just biological. I've learnt how to write my name in Chinese, and I've learnt bits of Shanghai's history. I have a walk every week in Xiangyang Park to see some old buildings from the French Concession period. My knowledge of architecture, however small it might be, has helped a lot." She looked at the minibus parked beside her. "My husband's company just organised an outing to Kunshan today. Our guide told us that Jiangsu Province alone is half the size of the UK."

"Mrs Wurman," he interrupted her. "Actually, I came to see you."

"Oh."

"I...I've noticed some things," he sighed. "That didn't quite add up."

"Yes?"

"There was a new filter in the Brita at Miss Peng's apartment." He thought for a while. "And her brother had arranged an autopsy. The contents in her stomach did not match the usual condiments used in a chain curry house. There were organic nutmeg and good-quality turmeric. Most of all, "he said, "she had a small cut on her finger. It matched the blood on the A4 paper she had left. The fingerprints on the codeine boxes were not quite the same." He smiled. "Did you know if you use liquid Band-Aid, it has the same effect as if using nail polish to conceal fingerprints? A cliché in many mystery books. On her mail that was delivered on the 4th, the fingerprints were still intact." He smiled again. "And I have also noticed that…you are of a similar size and height to her."

Tilly Wurman did not say anything.

"The lady who saw her for the last time – an employee from NP Properties – told me that Miss Peng had told her to update her contact details. I wondered why she did so when she had arranged to port her old number into a new network. I also checked her MacBook. She had printed a couple of documents along with the…the note she left. They are nowhere to be found."

He furrowed his brow as if annoyed by flies hovering over dinner. "So, I had a theory in mind. But not enough evidence. The apartment had already had a thorough cleaning." He looked away. The billboards of Hang Lung Plaza flaunted the latest designs from Paris, Tokyo, and New York.

"On another note," he said, "Sarnai – the cleaner who found Miss Peng's body with you – she's from Mongolia, and I grew up in Inner Mongolia. We had a nice chat reminiscing about our childhoods. Did you know that in Mongolia, if you step on someone's shoes from behind, the person in front has to turn and shake your hand, just to show that he or she holds no grudge?"

"She asked me if I had children. For that, I hated her."

Night had fallen.

He couldn't see Tilly Wurman. Or the expression on her face. The night air was muggy still, yet he felt he was slipping into a crevasse. He remembered Felipe saying that crocodile tears may be salty, but they also harbour problems.

He didn't know what had happened between the two of them. What he did know was that he had no right to imagine.

* * *

*Later.*

"Love is shellfish and bullshit," Felipe said, taking off his headphones. "Unlike some writers, I love to impose depression on my enemies. Have you ever read *The Price* by Arthur Miller?" He turned to Chance. "Everything is a business. Everything has a price. It's a pity that bullshit never had a market price as high as guano."

Felipe walked to the minibar and poured a glass of whiskey. "There are fifty shades of grey…And fifty ways to prey. Sara volunteers at a second-hand book shop, and they are bothered by an excessive donation of that book. Did you know that lamprey is a fish that has no scales, fins, or gill covers? More like a person without a heart and lungs. I hope my analogy is not flawed. Do you think we should find the cardiologist who performed on Tilly Wurman and ask if any slip-ups turned her so cold-hearted? She even added aspirin to that curry of hers. A signature dish, one might say." He smiled. "When you asked me that night in London whether I suspected if it was not a suicide, I said no. Because I did not 'suspect'; I knew it was not."

Felipe took up his glass. "Lies are like Shoji screens, for they break easily with a poke. Did she think she could pull off a James Bond pastiche? I had fine-combed that apartment like they would groom the Queen's corgis. And boy, did she fuck up. Amateur hour indeed. Murdering is a field where there is a chasm between theory and practice. Tilly Wurman, like any golfer, obviously needed to improve her lie." He took a sip and smiled again. "A man with a chronic illness learns to become a half-doctor. An avid bookworm knows how to pick up discords in others' narratives. Did she have such faith in the signal reception in the London Underground that she left no voicemails? Is that how one normally behaves when desperately trying to reach another?"

"Tell me what will happen," Chance said sternly.

"You did your part. Now it's time I do mine." Felipe grinned. "The brother had handpicked the deluxe option."

"Tell me."

"Oh, I don't want to ruin your appetite for *menudo* forever. Life's not like debugging; knowing where it went wrong won't make you happier."

"Tell me," he insisted.

"Urban legend has it that if you wish to torture someone the old way, you'll find a basement, tie your targets to some nice, sturdy chairs bolted to the floor with strong rivets," Felipe sat down on the leather sofa, "then put a few rats inside." He smiled. "What harm could a little Mickey Mouse do? You will know when you start pumping water into that basement. The rats, so desperate to survive, could burrow holes in certain objects and eventually pull out the guts. Trust me. They'll be in good hands." Felipe put down his glass.

"They?"

"The husband could do with a little time away as well." Felipe grinned again. "A vacation to the Caribbean, maybe. Too bad that they don't have children, or I could be more…creative in my planning. Have you ever heard of a pudding called 'baby's head'?" He hummed the tune of 'Sloop John B'.

Chance waited.

"Thanks to Sara, now whenever I come across a company, I do my due diligence…diligently. It seems the husband had led some drug trials in India that have, let's say, not achieved the desired treatment and brought on some unpleasant side effects. Poor rural girls would willingly undergo a trial if they had a few extra dollars of pocket money every month. And sometimes, they were not asked for their consent. Who would bother to translate the forms into regional dialects? The world could do with me doing more than one good deed a day. I'll allow you two more questions."

"What did you mean by you scratching my back?"

"I needed to curry favour with someone who could make the coroner overlook this case as a suicide. In exchange, I helped them to watch a *particular* someone's smoke."

Chance swallowed. "Was Alexander Roxborough part of this?"

"Oh. If I tell you yes, will you believe me? If I tell you no, will you believe me? Johnson once told you only to believe a third of what I say. Make it a tenth."

Felipe turned on the TV.

The news showed a Chinese celebrity couple shopping in a supermarket.

"I was very close to being engaged once," Felipe commented. "Not long before I found out, my future father-in-law had spearheaded a public health campaign in Peru. You know, I'm sure that my mother would never understand my current line of work. You may call it 'wild justice', even manufactured karma*." He crossed his legs. "I'm so glad now. The *batsu-ichis** could never outfox us when it comes to courting. Do remind me to send for Sara to join us in Shanghai. She could really make my blood sing."

Felipe turned his attention to Chance. "To borrow from an old Chinese saying, even the best banquets shall end. We made a good team. I have learnt from you, and I hope I have taught you well. I hope you will not be a fixed point in a changing age. It's all chaos out there, chaos not *ciaos*. Barbarians are not only at the gate, but they are also next door, or even in the same room, eating at the same table with you. It's fine to be merciless, and it's ok to be kind. The worst is to stuck in the middle. Care kills the cat." He grinned. "Don't forget to invite me to the wedding. I still look forward to meeting your stepmother. But I wouldn't hold any grudge if you didn't."

Felipe did not wait for Chance's reply.

"It's such a shame that we missed the cricket. I should have seen Jeremy Bentham's body at UCL and the Garden of Tranquillity in Hyde Park as well. Maybe we could watch the games together here? No, perhaps not; I've had enough of the British accent today." He took the remote control, changed the channel, and lost himself in *SpongeBob*.

Chance made himself a cup of tea.

There was no salt in the room.

He sat at the table intended for ten and looked out of the window.

The Oriental Pearl Tower still shone, and he felt a sudden rush of vertigo. He knew it would be a dreamless night for some and sleepless for some others.

\* \* \*

*October.*

London did not greet An with the same fervour as when she had visited in May.

For one, her mother had decided to send her a rice cooker. Customs detained it, and they had asked her to pay a clearing tariff higher than the original cost of the thing. She had decided to wait out until the parcel returned when payment was overdue.

The rain had also left her a little homesick.

She'd remembered that a classmate on her summer course said that there were only two true seasons in London: three months of spring and summer and nine months of autumn and winter.

An crossed the Waterloo Bridge in a drizzle.

Three boys parkoured around the entrance of an Underground station.

The cleaners at LSE were still striking. She could hear the distant sounds of protest made by vuvuzela. She found her way to the Strand Building. Someone was sitting on a bench, eating a homemade lunch. It smelled like curry.

An folded her umbrella, put it in its cover, and glimpsed through the various leaflets on the bulletin boards in the corridor connecting Strand Building and King's Building.

As a child, she and her brother liked to peruse the noticeboards in their neighbourhood and recount any news to their grandmother, who couldn't read very well, on their way from school.

An checked the floor map and found her way to the room for her programme orientation.

She was early.

Her uncle often said that early is on time and on time is late. She remembered.

A young girl with green hair leaned against the wall. She chewed a piece of gum as her fingers busied with her phone.

"Are you here for the course thing?" she looked up and asked.

"Yes. For the orientation."

The girl hesitated, "Umm…" She pointed in An's direction. "Would you like…"

"No. Thank you. I have already signed up for some societies."

The girl smiled. "No. I mean…look."

An looked down.

A rat scuttled away by her sneakers.

She jumped like a cat who had seen a cucumber.

"Don't worry," the girl laughed, "you'll get used to it. They say that you're only six feet away from a rat in London at any time."

\* \* \*

Catherine had a strange dream last night.

She had dreamt of Mr Darcy, playing with a glob of light blue fire.

The half-bottle of vodka sat untouched on her kitchen shelf.

Perhaps she still clung to a faint hope.

*Faint like that blue fire.*

She woke up, gathered her things, and rushed to her afternoon shift at the flower academy.

Melody, the head of the academy, had kept some lovely blossoming oleanders in one of the floral coolers. Orla, the new girl who had joined recently, stood beside their workstation.

"We always bump into big shots," Orla said as she cut the stems off some carnations. "He saw Renée Zellweger in a restaurant in Camden last time. Told me that she ordered several heavy dishes. My, my! How do they manage their bodies like that? Whew! Then I heard that *BJ3* was coming up. She did it for her role. And I saw an actress from *Black Mirror*…the first season, I think…in a Tesco's. We also went to the pub where they shot *Man Up*…Do you know that it's not actually in Shoreditch but Soho?"

Catherine listened as she sorted some ribbons.

Someone pressed the call bell.

She put down the ribbons, found a stapler to secure them, and walked towards the front counter.

Someone stood there.

"Good evening, Miss Roxborough."

She steadied herself.

*Two can play at this game.*

"Oh, Mr Yang! What a delight! How can I help you today?"

He smiled fleetingly. "I was hoping to get some flowers."

"Very well. And what might the occasion be?" Catherine asked all business-like while pretending to check the time on the till. "A romantic one, perhaps?"

"Umm…I couldn't say, really." He looked down.

"I thought you were quite good at noticing things?"

He looked up and smiled again. "I did notice certain…sparks. But I dare not to assert." He paused. "If all goes well, perhaps I could get some white roses to celebrate a new beginning." His eyes shone.

"I'm afraid, Mr Yang," Catherine sighed, "you are quite late. We have sold out of white roses for today."

"I see." He gave her a wan smile.

"And I'm seeing someone later."

"Oh." His eyes dimmed, and his shoulders slumped. "I…I better not…I better get going."

*Gotcha!*

Catherine walked out from behind the counter. "Now, tell me, Mr Yang. Where were you when I caught a cold last month? I was hoping to try some

Chinese remedies. I've heard that they work."

He smiled again, more wistfully this time. "I guess…I was quitting my last job, and I needed some time to renew my visa to come to the UK." He laughed lightly and shrugged. "Not my favourite pastime."

"Do you plan to stay for long this time?" Catherine eyed the clock on the wall once again.

"Well…Miss Roxborough, I better not delay you anymore." He turned and then turned back. "Goodbye, then."

"Wait!" Catherine called out.

He turned back once again, slowly, his eyes dreading and entreating.

She saw a glint of hope, hope for new beginnings, in his eyes.

She waited for a few heartbeats and smiled warmly. "I've already made plans with Cecil tonight, but I can call him to say that I have a…friend in town."

He let out the breath he'd been holding.

"Very well. Perhaps we could go to Vanilla Black? I took the liberty of reserving a table for two." He noticed the time. "I see your shift is not over yet. I will wait on the bench outside."

"Good." Catherine walked up to him. "Now that you are here, I would very much like to keep you in my sight."

They embraced.

Outside, a child walked by with an orange balloon in her hand.

# EPILOGUE

## 2009

C ontrary to popular belief, London in July was no place for a pleasant
visit.

Nor a stay.

The piazza in front of North Kensington Tube Station teemed with
passers-by.

Lynette Sun sat on a rattan chair at an outdoor café, looking at the
golden ring of fire burning in the porcelain blue sky through her wide-
brimmed hat.

*Qué calor…*

She picked up a menu from the round glass table and fanned it, swirling
a warm blast of air onto her face.

How thoughtless of her to have forgotten to pack her portable electric fan.

"Gemme two icy coffee." A man settled down two tables away and
shouted to a waiter.

He had a corbeau tank, revealing a sunburnt neck, not unlike turkey. The
man took out a handkerchief and swiped beads of sweat off his balding
head. A soft breeze brought the scent of mint-based antiperspirant to
Lynette.

*Uf!*

Lynette shook her head as she watched the melee of people thronging the piazza as if she had seen a photo distorted with an impressionist filter.

It was well past three, but her date had yet to appear. She decided to put more sunscreen on her calves.

A familiar voice reached her a few minutes later.

"Sorry, I'm late. Had a little situation."

Lynette did not bother looking up. "You've forgotten your dad's famous saying, early is on time and on time is late. And late is…" She took a long sip from her glass. Her ice tea had grown tepid. She then shovelled her sunscreen into her handbag and stared at her stepson.

Chance was wearing a light blue Oxford shirt, a pair of black jeans, and matching sneakers. He looked at her with smiling eyes through his glasses.

Lynette noticed that one of the temples seemed strange. It made use of a piece of connecting tape.

He pulled out a chair and sat down. His right hand went to rub his back.

She knew it was the sequela from his traffic accident years ago that gave him trouble.

"Never mind," Lynette waved her hand. "Do tell me the programme that you had planned for us."

He glanced at the menu. "Isabel is still at work, so I made a reservation at the Sketch for eight. They have good food and delicate décor, especially the bathrooms. I think you'll like it. We still have plenty of time, and there's a lot to see around here. We could check out the V&A or the Natural History Museum, or we could go boat rowing in Hyde Park."

"Ha?" Lynette questioned with a squeak. "Rowing in this weather? Don't you think that I have suffered enough from this heat already? Aren't you afraid of me getting a heatstroke queuing in front of the museums?"

"I'm sure there are measures against that." He moved his hand under his chin. "If there's anywhere you'd like to go, just tell me, and we can go."

Lynette thought for a while. "This restaurant you mentioned, is it far from Oxford Street?"

"It's on Regent Street, a few blocks away from Oxford Circus Station – not that far at all."

"If the circumstances allow." Lynette pulled out her wallet and left a tenner on the silver plate resting on the table. She gathered her things quickly and stood up, holding her handbag. "Let's go shopping."

Isabel joined them halfway through dinner. The law firm she interned at was working on a large M&A case, and it was always the nobodies who carried the water for the office during these big times. Afterwards, they caught a cab and saw Isabel back at her workplace on Portugal Street.

The sun was still hiding behind rolls of clouds while the three of them stood in the shadows of a bricked office building and chatted.

Isabel said to him. "I have my bike here, and I'll go home when I'm done. You can have a nice evening with your *belle-mère*." She then waved goodbye to Lynette.

Lynette suggested an after-dinner stroll around the area. He led her through the campus of LSE, onto Aldwych, and finally turned to the junction at Waterloo Bridge.

Even the fiercest sun would set eventually.

The night finally began to fall after ten.

"Does that thing still work?"

A strong wind rushed through them, and Lynette collected her waist-long hair while casually pointing to the London Eye.

"Yes," he nodded. He checked the time on his phone. "But it's closed now. If you are interested, we could go early tomorrow. They have a huge queue; it's the summer holidays."

"Is that so?" Lynette turned to look east. The bankside over there was gloomy, but the outline of St Paul's Cathedral was clear. The pedestrian walkways by the river hosted many people. Their noises overflowed the rancid smell of the river. "We better not." She smiled, "Did you know that the Ferris Wheel was an invention with colonial implications? Besides, I don't want to be a silly tourist taking pictures with a small camera. Good scenery is best captured by heart."

Chance nodded lightly.

"So, how's life in the Great Wen?"

"Not bad."

"I'm surprised at your Spanish. You did exceed my expectations." Lynette laughed, "We have a new designer on board, and he spent three years in Barcelona. He only knows five words: 'holá, cerveza, el baño, gracias, adiós'."

"You made it sound like a flash fiction," he mused.

Lynette laughed for a long time.

✳ ✳ ✳

*A week later.*

He accompanied Lynette to the new terminal at Heathrow and helped her to check her bags in.

Before parting, she handed him a box. It was a watch.

And an expensive one, by the look of its packaging.

"Do you remember your dad's good teaching?" she asked.

He winced. "You know, I could really do with a nice video card."

Lynette froze for a moment. "Oh! I've forgotten. I shouldn't gift any watches…"

"That's fine. I'm not that superstitious." He received the box. "I even shared a pear last time. And thank you. I'll wear it for my graduation."

Lynette relaxed a little. "Will you do me a favour? Take care, and don't worry about your cat. He eats better than your dad."

He smiled. "Vale."

They hugged and parted.

He found his way to the Piccadilly Line; the tracks were still new.

Julian had sent him a message, asking if he could borrow his shirt stays.

He replied and read an ad above his head. It was a telecom ad.

The train passed through a tunnel. A wet piece of cemetery flew by, then another tunnel.

The lights inside flashed. He took out Lynette's present and opened it. There was a small note.

*Carry on and beat them all dead.*

He laughed.

Chance Yang was content.

He wondered what life had in store for him.

Some new beginnings. Maybe.

# Notes and Terms

**Chapter 3** – *otsukare* – Japanese greeting showing appreciation for one's hard work.

**Chapter 3** – 'When you regard the view from a bridge, others regard you as their view.' – Chance quotes from Bian Zhilin's *Fragment*.

**Chapter 4** – *yokai* – Japanese for supernatural creatures.

**Chapter 4** – *Todai* – Japanese for the abbreviation for the University of Tokyo.

**Chapter 4** – *nazotoki* – Japanese for the moment when a detective reveals who the murderer is in a book.

**Chapter 4** – *misaki* – Japanese for a headland.

**Chapter 4** – 'No need to sweat; the room has been thoroughly cleaned. If you still have doubts, bring some salt.' – In Japan, funeral attendees often throw salt on their shoulders once they reach home to repel evil spirits.

**Chapter 7** – *sexenio* – Spanish for a six-year term or cycle.

**Chapter 8** – 'Those out of the city want to come in; those in the city want an escape.' – Chance's inner thought based on *The Besieged City* by Qian Zhongshu.

**Chapter 8** – 'Doors are dangerous. They should be outlawed. Thankfully he didn't catch his neck in it.' – Felipe quotes James Bond from *Live and Let Die* by Ian Fleming.

**Chapter 8** – 'A Chinese writer once wrote that people's imagination runs so wild that as soon as they see short sleeves, they will think of bare arms, then nudity, then genitals, then the illegitimate child.' – Chance quotes from Lu Xun's collection of essays *And That's That.*

**Chapter 8** – *menudo* – Spanish for a soup made with cow's stomach and red chilli.

**Chapter 8** – 'Durkheim defines suicide as any death, which is the direct or indirect result of a positive or negative act accomplished by the victim himself.' – Felipe quotes from Durkheim, E. & Simpson, George, 2002. Suicide: A study in sociology, Hoboken: Routledge.

**Chapter 9** – *nominication* – Japanese for the act of communicating over drinks with subordinates and bosses.

**Chapter 9** – 'French fries, freedom fries...' – Felipe refers to an initiative in the US to change the name of French fries to 'freedom fries' when the French government did not support the US involvement in the Iraq war.

**Chapter 10** – 'His eyes were like tunnels; my first thought was that he had committed a crime.' – Felipe reads from *A View from the Bridge* by Arthur Miller

**Chapter 12** – 'Tupí or not Tupí? That's the Whites' burden.' – Felipe quotes from the *Cannibalist Manifesto* by Oswald de Andrade and refers to the phrase, 'a white man's burden'.

**Chapter 12** – *otsumami* – Japanese for a drinking snack.

**Chapter 12** – *inago* – Japanese for locusts.

**Chapter 12** – 'What do you think? Perhaps a teddy bear? And a card. What shall I write? How about: 'greetings from Minsk'?' – Felipe refers to the teddy bear incident in 2012 when some Swedish activists airdropped teddy bears with messages of advocacy in Minsk, the capital city of Belarus.

**Chapter 13** – 'You may call it 'wild justice'... even manufactured karma.' – Felipe refers to Francis Bacon's definition of revenge.

**Chapter 13** – *batsu-ichi* – Japanese for those who divorced their first spouse.

# A Chinese Remedy